A Candlelight
Ecstasy Romance®

**"I don't jump into bed with just anyone,"
she reasoned.**

"Do you think I'm just anyone, Kalinda? I know
you like me," Gavin insisted.

"You're pretty sure of yourself, aren't you?" she
countered.

"A man knows these things about a woman," he
answered smugly. "Look, I know you're attracted
to me but I just don't know why you won't do anything about it. Being intimate with someone can be
a very beautiful experience."

Kalinda glared at him. "I'm not looking simply
for a beautiful experience, Gavin. I want something
more lasting."

"Well, how do you know we can't have something lasting unless you give us a chance?"

He was right, but how did she know those
weren't just words to get her into bed, that he
wasn't just offering her a casual fling?

A CANDLELIGHT ECSTASY ROMANCE®

One in a Million

Joan Grove

A CANDLELIGHT ECSTASY ROMANCE®

Published by
Dell Publishing Co., Inc.
1 Dag Hammarskjold Plaza
New York, New York 10017

Dell ® TM 681510, Dell Publishing Co., Inc.

Candlelight Ecstasy Romance®, 1,203,540, is a registered
trademark of Dell Publishing Co., Inc., New York, New York.

ISBN: 0-440-16664-0

Printed in the United States of America

First printing—October 1984

For my mom and dad and my son, Christian. And for those who have made this book possible: Anne, Kelle, and a special thanks to Lydia for all of her endless faith and guidance.

To Our Readers:

We have been delighted with your enthusiastic response to Candlelight Ecstasy Romances®, and we thank you for the interest you have shown in this exciting series.

In the upcoming months we will continue to present the distinctive, sensuous love stories you have come to expect only from Ecstasy. We look forward to bringing you many more books from your favorite authors and also the very finest work from new authors of contemporary romantic fiction.

As always, we are striving to present the unique, absorbing love stories that you enjoy most—books that are more than ordinary romance.

Your suggestions and comments are always welcome. Please write to us at the address below.

Sincerely,

The Editors
Candlelight Romances
1 Dag Hammarskjold Plaza
New York, New York 10017

CHAPTER ONE

It was mid-December and the promise of a severe winter in New York was in the air. Kalinda clutched the collar of her beige cashmere coat in an effort to keep out the brutal, cutting wind as her long brown hair floated around her face. Her steps were brisk as she hurried toward Alan Richards's office, nestled high atop a posh building on Fifth Avenue and Fifty-third Street.

Up the gleaming elevator, out into the hallway, Kalinda faced the bold, gold-inscribed letters: *Alan Richards Ltd.* The reception area was incredible, the most magnificent Kalinda had ever seen, with its exotic plants, chrome furniture mixed with antiques, an original Remington painting, and a Tiffany lamp that was set on the receptionist's desk.

At the breathtaking sight Kalinda's steps faltered. This was one of the most exciting days of her life, and she looked forward to meeting the famous designer and discussing all the ideas she had for his luggage line. Taking a seat, she waited for her name to be announced. The seconds seemed like an eternity until she heard—

"All right, Ms. Forrest, Mr. Richards can see you now. Right this way."

Kalinda smiled appreciatively and followed the tall woman's quick steps. She was led through a long white corridor, past many offices, until at last she arrived at Alan Richards's office. His secretary opened the door and a panorama of Central Park greeted her. To Kalinda's right, behind a well-polished oak desk, sat Alan Richards, the trend-setting designer. His hair was jet black and his face had a chiseled effect with strong, evenly proportioned features. He looked more handsome and dignified than in any of the photographs Kalinda had seen of him in fashion magazines. But he seemed too neat, too perfect.

"Kalinda, it's great to meet you. I can finally put a face to the voice on the phone," he declared the moment he saw her.

Kalinda smiled and returned pleasantly, "Thank you, Alan. I'm glad all the phone calls paid off. It's a pleasure to meet you."

Lines formed at the corners of his mouth as a grin spread across his face. Kalinda removed her gloves and opened her coat.

Standing, his pinstripe suit fitting his slender body like a glove, Alan quickly walked over to Kalinda. "Let me help you. It really is cold, isn't it?" he asked, helping her slip out of her coat, sliding back a mirrored door, and hanging it in the closet.

"Yes, it is," she responded, rubbing her cold hands together. "I walked over from my office."

"That's some walk!" he said, surprised.

12

"Oh, I rather enjoyed it," Kalinda said. "And anyway, I wanted the time to go over the ideas I have for the new line."

"Grace warned me you'd be anxious to start. Won't you sit down," Alan offered, indicating the black leather chair next to his desk. They both sat.

"I don't know if you know," Alan began, "but Grace went to school with my wife's mother and we've been friends for a long time. She's such a special person and when she mentioned she had someone she wanted us to meet at her Christmas party and that you were in the premium business—well, I couldn't wait until Christmas. Especially since I was in the market for a manufacturer for my new luggage line. By the way, have you seen Grace lately?"

"No, I haven't," she replied quickly. "I haven't been to Martha's Vineyard in ages. But we've talked a lot on the phone and I will be going to her party." It is amazingly fortunate, she thought, that Grace knew the Richardses. If she got the job and became the licensee for his luggage line, her company would be established once and for all.

"Well, I'm certain I'll see you there." Then he was silent for a moment, as though going over his thoughts. He leaned forward in his chair and Kalinda automatically moved closer to him. "Kalinda," he said softly, as though sharing a secret, "there'll be a few other companies bidding on the job and I always try to be fair, but I have to admit I'm going to give you the edge. Just come up with good quality and a fair price, and you'll get the job."

Kalinda shook her head and smiled appreciatively. "I can't believe that you'd give my company this chance. My partner and I will definitely do everything we can to justify your faith in us. I'm sure you'll love Kate's designs and my sales pitch."

"No doubt about it." He smiled with acknowledgment. "Well, let's get down to business." Pushing his finger down on the button, he spoke into the intercom. "Miss Reid, please have Gavin come into my office."

At the sound of this Gavin's name, Kalinda sat back in her chair, wondering why she would be meeting someone else.

Noticing the puzzled look on her face, Alan explained, "Gavin is my brother and the business genius in the family. I want him to work closely with you."

"Does this mean I won't be working with you?" Kalinda asked with an edge of disappointment in her voice.

"I trust his judgment implicitly," Alan continued enthusiastically, totally unaware of Kalinda's disappointment. "Even though I'd love to work on the new line with you, Kalinda, I can't. I'm too busy right now with a deadline for some new designs. By the way, what is your delivery time?"

"Approximately a hundred and twenty days, once the design has been approved." She quoted the terms by rote because delivery time was the most vital part of her business and usually the first question prospective clients asked.

"That's good." Alan seemed genuinely pleased. "I want the line in the department stores by late September or early October. It's a bit of a rush. Can we get samples soon?"

"Yes, we'll have several samples made up. Probably within two to three weeks after we come up with the designs." Her words had been strung together—the realization that the project was almost hers had stimulated

14

Kalinda's creative energies, leaving this Gavin fellow forgotten for the moment.

"I know there's a lot of work to be done, but I'm hoping that you will come through, Kalinda. I have the feeling," Alan stated, nodding and giving her a knowing look, "that you can do it."

"Thank you, Alan. I'm going to do my best to prove you right."

Kalinda heard footsteps. Turning, her brown eyes focused upon the man standing in the doorway. There was nothing especially attractive about him. In fact, he was quite ordinary looking, despite his red hair and the fact that he was at least six foot three. He certainly couldn't be related to Alan. Their eyes suddenly met. His were blue and had a sharpness about them that she had encountered before in only the most calculating and shrewd of men. He emanated power, quiet, controlled power, which Kalinda knew could be deadly. And Kalinda was aware that he might have understood her reaction to him.

"Kalinda," she heard Alan say as she turned back to him, welcoming the interruption. "I'd like you to meet my brother Gavin."

She responded to Alan's introduction with a smile and a nod, waiting a moment before she faced his brother again.

"Hello, Gavin," she said in a friendly tone.

"Hello," he replied in a deep, manly voice. "You're the woman who has the premium business, right?"

"Yes, I am," she returned assuredly.

"Alan told me I'd be working on the project with you. Couldn't be more pleased," he stated as he strolled in with strong, confident steps, his hands hidden in the pockets of his gray flannel pants. His blue eyes glared at her, then traveled down her slender neck and appeared to stop at the V neck of her lavender coatdress while she stared at the top of his carrot head. Kalinda refused to check out *where* he was looking, but the back of her neck bristled. She had a full bosom and a little cleavage *was* showing. Damn him! Automatically she crossed her legs and then caught herself—a Freudian slip, no doubt, she mused.

The carrot top moved and he was now looking into her face. There was an amused gleam in his eyes; probably hawkeye had picked up on her discomfort. He smiled!

"Not as pleased as I am. I'm going to enjoy working with you, Gavin." Her voice had a forced quality and Kalinda prayed Alan hadn't picked up on her underlying sarcasm.

"Well, I'm sure the two of you will work fine together," Alan said with a faint trace of amusement.

Had Alan caught his brother's roaming eye? Kalinda laughed, more in nervous relief than anything else, and stated, "I'm certain we can, Alan." Then she smiled sweetly at Gavin.

An amorous grin spread across Gavin's face as he eyed Kalinda mischievously. Her cheeks flushed and she turned her eyes toward Alan.

"Gavin will discuss all the ideas we have for the line," Alan explained, his face now serious, "the type of fabric and colors for the luggage. And he can help with manufacturing suggestions if you need them."

He glanced at his watch and rose quickly. "I'm sorry, but I have an appointment in ten minutes. Last-minute details. Good-bye, Kalinda. I'll see you soon."

"Great, Alan," Kalinda replied in a quiet tone, disappointed that he was leaving.

Alan smiled at Kalinda, then tapped his brother on the shoulder. "I'll catch you later."

Gavin nodded. Alan looked at one and then the other before taking his coat and rushing out the door.

Kalinda stared down at her hands. It bothered her to be alone with him. The thought of working with him came to mind and she frowned. Business genius, huh? He seemed more a womanizer than a business tycoon. She hoped she wouldn't be spending her time keeping his mind off her body and on the luggage. She also hoped he wasn't the type who wanted a say in everything because Kalinda couldn't work that way. She needed a free hand when developing a new product. She looked up with doubt on her face. He was staring down at her—his eyes bluer than she had first thought—one unruly blond hair from his eyebrow straying upward. He looked like a cute, overgrown boy, and Kalinda suddenly felt strangely vulnerable.

"How about dinner tonight?" he asked softly as he leaned over toward her.

Just as I thought, she mused knowingly.

"Sorry, I can't," Kalinda returned, too quickly. Then, not wanting to offend him—this was business, after all— she added, "I already have plans. But how about lunch tomorrow?"

"Too rushed," he stated abruptly, still hovering over her.

"What?" Kalinda snapped—she hadn't expected *that* reaction.

"Lunch is too rushed. We need more time. I have a lot to discuss. Dinner would be much better."

Kalinda didn't miss the implication of what that meant and again distrusted his motives.

17

"I prefer lunch," she said determinedly. Lunch is more businesslike and safer, Kalinda added silently to herself.

"I don't bite if that's what you think, Kalinda," he said patronizingly, as if he had read her mind.

"How can I be sure—I only have *your* word for it!" Kalinda shot back, disliking his condescending attitude. But instantly annoyed that she had lost her professional poise, she inhaled and calmly said, "Dinner will be fine. Tomorrow night?"

Gavin frowned, not missing the coolness in her response. "Your enthusiasm is overwhelming."

"A restaurant of your choice," she stated, ignoring his remark.

"Do you know where Lutèce is?"

Hearing that he wanted to take her to one of the most elegant restaurants in New York, Kalinda suddenly felt that maybe she had misjudged him. "Yes, of course," she managed in a soft voice.

"Most fantastic food."

"You're correct about that," she murmured.

"They have the best escargots in town."

"Yes, they do," she returned in a slightly breathy voice. Kalinda could almost taste the wonderful sauce with all that garlic. "It's my favorite."

"Mine too," he said warmly with a smile. Kalinda softened and smiled back sincerely. "Well, the restaurant we're going to is right down the street from there—Damiens. On Fiftieth and the east side of First. Can't miss it," he said matter-of-factly, sitting on the corner of Alan's desk, draping one leg over it.

Kalinda was furious at him for toying with her that way. She muttered in disbelief, "What was the name you mentioned?"

18

"Damiens," he repeated.

But Kalinda hardly heard him. And I was ashamed of the way I judged him! And I foolishly thought he would take me to a restaurant like Lutèce! Kalinda, you're crackers! A horrid impulse to yank out a clump of his red hair came to mind, but instead she glared at him, seething inside.

"You don't like the place?" he asked in a disappointed tone.

"I don't *know* the place," she returned coolly.

"Oh, . . . well, you'll really like it. It's my favorite restaurant," he said with what appeared to be a genuine smile.

Kalinda studied him for a moment, wondering if this had been his idea of a joke. She glanced down at the floor —it was time to go. "I have to leave. I'm looking forward to seeing you tomorrow," she lied as she stood up abruptly.

"Honesty is the best policy, Ms. Forrest."

"I agree, Gavin. Let's shake on it. After all, we do have to *work* together," she stressed, letting him know that would be *all* they would be doing together. She offered her hand, which was taken into a larger, very masculine one, and held too tightly. For some reason Gavin had a way of getting under her skin; Kalinda quickly withdrew her hand from his grasp.

"See you tomorrow," she said, moving quickly to the mirrored door and getting her coat.

"Let me help you." He gallantly took the coat from her and held it while she eased into it. There was a scent of cologne, a pleasant, not overbearing aroma—probably Kanon. Funny, he seemed like a spicy Brut man, Kalinda thought sarcastically to herself.

19

"I'll call you tomorrow," he whispered into her ear. His hands stayed on her collar longer than she liked and she inched away from him.

"Fine," Kalinda returned as she reached the door then disappeared into the safety of the hallway.

Once out of the building and Alan Richards's office, Kalinda refused to give Gavin a second thought. If Alan was a prince, his brother was a frog and she'd deal with him in her own way.

As she walked briskly down the street, Kalinda didn't feel her feet hitting the pavement or the cold wind hitting her face. Now her thoughts were on the future success of her company and her struggle to get where she was today.

Shortly after her divorce from Grace's son, her parents were killed in a plane crash, leaving Kalinda terribly alone and frightened. She had been thrust into a new and terrifying life-style, single and jobless. She had never planned on a career, but being the survivor she was, Kalinda quickly secured a job in New York City in the premium business. It was a small office with just her and her boss. As the only salesperson, she contacted cosmetic companies, trying to sell them gift-with-purchase promotional items such as bags, umbrellas, and mugs. Adept at learning the ins and outs of the business, she was bringing in huge sales for the company within a very short time. Unfortunately, her unscrupulous, greedy boss attempted to hold back her commission, and finally, when he tried to pass off inferior materials as quality products to make bigger profits, it was the last straw for Kalinda. Her reputation was at stake, so she walked away with half his business by taking her clients with her and started her own company with her close friend Kate.

Now she had the opportunity of a lifetime—to establish their company once and for all. Alan Richards was one of the most respected and sought-after designers in the world. Their connection with him as his luggage licensee would make their company famous.

Kalinda moved with quicker, more determined steps. She would get that account. Kate and she would work harder than they ever had before, and nothing and no one would stand in their way of coming up with the best design and price. She would handle carrot top—*Big Red* —she laughed to herself. She would find a way. If she could just keep in mind that she only had to deal with him for a short time. And the first thing she would do when she got back to her office—except, of course, to fill Kate in on all the details—would be to call Grace and thank her, letting her know how well the meeting with Alan went and how much she looked forward to her party.

The cold didn't exist for Kalinda because she was warmed by all the excitement. And no wonder she couldn't remember her feet touching the pavement—she was flying.

The next day Kalinda's head throbbed. A disastrous problem had been discovered with a new shipment of bags from the Orient. The buttons on the bags had been corroded by dampness that accumulated when the poly shipping bags were sealed. The phone did nothing but ring, their receptionist was out with the flu, and tonight Kalinda had to go out with Gavin!

Kate sat across from her, studying a shipping schedule and taking a deep drag on her cigarette, a gray cloud of smoke encircling her. Kate was always the optimistic

21

one, always so cheerful. Kalinda couldn't ever remember a time when her friend sounded negative, not even when they first met in college. And Kate was so damned independent. But Kalinda loved her all the more for it.

Kalinda cringed as the phone rang. "Oh, no, not again!" she exclaimed.

"Relax. I'll get it," Kate offered lightly. "Hello, this is the Bag Lab. . . . Yes, she is. Just a moment please." Kate pushed the hold button down and turned with an impish expression upon her face. "Guess who?"

Kalinda shook her weary head. "I give up. Who?"

Kate smiled and her eyes sparkled with anticipation. "Mr. Richards . . . Gavin Richards, that is," she declared in a clear, sharp voice—too sharp for Kalinda's aching head.

"Oh, great! Isn't there some way I can get out of it? Wouldn't you like to go in my place, Kate?" Her brown eyes pleaded for help.

"No way, José. The guy is all yours and it's not polite to keep him waiting. Don't forget this is a big account." Kate shook the phone like some foreboding object. "Just keep in mind, it's business."

Kalinda sighed deeply. "Thanks a lot."

"You're more than welcome," Kate teased back.

Kalinda groaned as she took the phone and released the hold button.

"Hello, Gavin, sorry to keep you waiting. I was in the middle of something," she stated in a dull tone.

"No problem," his deep voice returned. "How's eight? I'll pick you up."

"You don't waste any time, do you? I like that—a man of action," Kalinda quipped. "Yes, I'm sure I'll be finished by then."

Kalinda glanced at her friend and signaled again for help, but Kate shook her head as Kalinda answered, "I'll meet you at the restaurant when I'm through here."

Gavin asked cheerfully, "Remember the name of the place?"

"How could I forget?" Her blood started to boil all over again. "It's right down from Lutèce—you know, that elegant place with the best escargots in town," she returned, mimicking his deep, masculine voice. "Damiens, right?"

"Right! See you then," Gavin returned warmly. Then there was a click. Kalinda held the receiver to her ear a moment longer before dropping it back on the hook.

"You must be joking," Kate said dryly.

Kalinda looked sharply over at her partner, wondering what she meant.

"He's taking *you* to *Damiens?*" Kate asked, trying to suppress her laughter. Kalinda nodded with trepidation. "That's where all the animals meet," Kate declared with an outrageous laugh, which thoroughly peeved Kalinda.

"See, I told you that you should go. You're great handling that element," Kalinda jabbed wickedly.

"And you're not? I saw the glint in your eye when I mentioned animals. And let me tell you, honey, you've got a live one on your hands!"

"That's why I call him Big Red!" Kalinda returned quickly without missing a beat.

"Well, you better watch out. You may just end up liking him."

Kalinda's brow furrowed. "What makes you say that?"

Kate smiled her charming way. "Something about the way your face lit up when I said his name. Anyway, hope

23

you have a good time. You should *always* have a good time, Kalinda," Kate said teasingly.

"I agree, Kate." Kalinda studied her partner for a moment, then added, "But I'm not going for a good time. This is business."

"Well, you can make a good time out of it. Have fun landing the job and you might get to know a nice guy in the process. It could turn out to be quite interesting."

"I have no interest in him, despite what you think, except what he can do for me—for the both of us. That's it." And I will keep that in mind, Kalinda silently promised herself.

"You're too serious, Kalinda. Haven't you heard the old saying, you may meet Mr. Right when you're out with Mr. Wrong. What have you got to lose?"

Kalinda laughed. "Kate, you have an answer for everything. I'm not expecting to find what I'm looking for at Damiens or with Gavin. But I'll keep in mind what you said about meeting Mr. Right while I'm out with Big Red tonight. With my luck though, Mr. Right will probably arrive at the door and because he's on a white charger, the bouncer won't let him in!"

Kalinda giggled as Kate joined in appreciatively.

Finally Kalinda asked, "Now that that's settled, what are we going to do about the corroded buttons?"

Kate thought a moment, then declared, "Pull out the Yellow Pages. Maybe we can dig up a company to put new ones on."

"That's a good idea. Let my fingers do the walking."

"Clever. Clever. And I'll call the client. He may know someone who can do it," Kate stated. "Besides, we'd better get the rest of the work done; I don't want you late for your hot date tonight. By the way, why didn't you want

24

him to pick you up at your apartment? Afraid he might have more than business in mind?" Kate added with delight, raising the brows over her blue eyes and placing a hand on her short, curly black hair.

"You really must think me a prude!" Kalinda retorted with a laugh. Kate nodded with a grin. "Well," Kalinda continued with a toss of her head, "excuse me, but *I* have work to do." Her words were spoken in a terrible imitation of an English accent, but her humor was short-lived. Kate's question reminded her again of her own apprehension when Gavin had insisted upon dinner. What if Mr. Gavin Richards had something other than business in mind? Well if he did, she thought determinedly, he was in for one hell of a surprise!

CHAPTER TWO

Kalinda squinted as her eyes adjusted to the dimly lit room. Her cheeks, still stinging from the cold wind, were hit with a blast of hot air, smoke, and jukebox music. Men standing four deep at the bar blocked her entrance. Her brown eyes anxiously scanned the place for Gavin. Luckily, with his height and red hair, he *did* stand out in a crowd. Exhausting her efforts, Kalinda frowned. He wasn't there. A group of people came in behind her and she was pushed forward. Men surrounded her. Some had their eyes glued to the hockey game on a TV at the end of the bar and were cheering for the New York Rangers. Others were involved in business chatter or heated political debates. A few gave Kalinda the once-over. When would they grow up?

She disliked bars, especially crowded bars, and would never have come into one by herself. The men always had that predatory look in their eyes. She should have had Gavin pick her up. Better yet, she should have canceled the meeting!

26

Standing on tiptoe, she strained to see the dining area. There was an opening off to her right past the end of the bar, adorned with brown curtains pulled off to the side and trimmed with a plastic Tiffany design. Perhaps that's where Gavin was. Kalinda took off in that direction.

Trying to squeeze past two burly men, Kalinda said in an exasperated voice, "Excuse me! Please!"

"That's okay, honey. Want a drink?" someone called after her.

Kalinda quickened her steps, spurred on by anger, as she pushed through the crowd. Finally she reached her destination. The decor was something out of the Prohibition era. The walls and ceiling were decorated with pendants from various colleges, pro teams, and counties of Ireland. Framed clippings about sports events hung everywhere. Two television sets at opposite ends of the room were tuned to the same channel—the hockey game. The place appeared to be a hangout for sports enthusiasts —no, sports *fanatics!* So, thought Kalinda after studying the patrons, Gavin isn't even in here, what I will *loosely* call the dining room. God, what did I do to deserve this! she added, shaking her head.

Hot and exhausted, with the threat of her headache returning, Kalinda would have given anything to have her hands on him, especially around his neck. The idea of having him at her mercy while she imagined her fingers slowly strangling him reactivated her adrenal glands. The thought of it made her chuckle. Then, remembering where she was, Kalinda quickly raised her shoulders and lowered her head, looking sheepishly around to see if anyone had noticed. They probably think I'm nuts laughing to myself. Kalinda frowned. But in this place the crazies are, no doubt, welcomed with open arms.

27

Feeling a little better and remembering that she was there on business, very important business—trapped in other words—Kalinda pulled off her gloves with an authoritative jerk as she waited, trying to catch a waiter's eye.

Finally one came to her rescue. "Can I help you?" the little, spectacled man posed in a thick Irish brogue.

"Yes, is Gavin Richards here?" she said, totally frustrated.

"No, not yet," the man said with a shake of his red hair, "but we have his favorite table reserved."

"I'm glad to hear that," Kalinda replied with a smile, looking forward to escaping the crush of the men at the bar.

"Yes, the most popular booth we have. You can sit there and watch the TV and at the same time keep an eye on the entrance for Mr. Richards."

Kalinda laughed—the irony of it!

"Knew you'd like it, miss!" he declared, leading the way.

"It's a terrific idea," she quipped back as they reached the table. Kalinda removed her coat before easing into the black vinyl seat facing the entrance.

"Sit back and relax and enjoy yourself. You know, as we say in the old country, 'When God created time, he made plenty of it.' Can I get you anything, miss?" he asked as Kalinda looked into two elfish eyes.

"Yes, a glass of Chablis and some water please," she responded before the little man disappeared.

Kalinda glanced at her watch. Five minutes to eight. She had been early; he wasn't late. She breathed deeply. Why had Gavin bothered her so? She did find him unattractive, didn't she? Restlessly she jabbed at her napkin with the fork.

She surveyed the room again and Kate's words "That's where all the animals meet" came to mind. She'd been accurate. It was a typical jock bar. If only I were meeting with Alan, Kalinda mused to herself, I would probably be seated at Lutèce or perhaps The Four Seasons right now. How could that oaf think of talking business in here!

The waiter interrupted her thoughts as he appeared with the glasses and placed them before her. Kalinda drank the water first—six glasses a day was part of her strict diet. The diet had been the first step toward her program to become more polished. It had been hard work to shed the old image of her happy-go-lucky college days. But she found it was needed to give her the edge in business deals. Clients seemed to be more impressed with her sleek new look, seemed to trust what they were familiar with. It had been hard work—the exercise classes after work, the endless trips to the beauty salon for hair straightening, manicures, facials, and makeup consultations, and the constant entertaining of clients. She placed the empty glass back down as clippings about sports events stared up at her from under the laminated table-top.

As Kalinda raised her head she saw Gavin looking at her from across the room, an enigmatic smile upon his face. The expression in his eyes drew hers so that Kalinda could not look away from him. For an instant she was touched by his look and saw beneath the surface of Gavin Richards. It was the glimpse of a more exciting and appealing man, and Kalinda was confused, even bothered, by what she saw. His sudden movement toward her

29

broke the spell. Kalinda quickly lowered her eyes and put out of her mind the way this man had suddenly but deeply affected her.

Kalinda mechanically raised the glass of wine to her lips, hardly tasting the cool, refreshing Chablis, and slowly replaced it on the table. Her fingers felt the contour of the stem while her eyes stared down at the translucent liquid. There was a stirring next to her and Kalinda knew Gavin had arrived. She looked up. The big G on his Gucci belt caught her eye as Gavin removed his coat. Plaid lining, the trademark of a Burberry raincoat, could be seen, bringing a smile to Kalinda's face. After all her years here, she still couldn't get used to the trench coat as the official winter uniform of the businessman in New York City. Where she was from, a raincoat was for the rain and a more substantial coat was worn in the winter.

"Been here long?" he asked, his blue eyes smiling down at her, his coat folded across his arms.

"No, not at all," Kalinda replied in a quiet, pleasant tone. Still shaken by the effect he had upon her, the anger she felt earlier was put in cold storage for the moment.

"Now isn't this better than that other snobby place up the block? I know it has pretty good food, but you can't relax there," he stated nonchalantly, without any hint of malice, as he hung his coat on the hook ne. to the booth.

Kalinda was baffled. She knew he was referring to Lutèce but could he be serious? Relax? In this saloon? Just then a roar went up from the crowd and Kalinda jumped. Gavin turned in the direction of the noise, facing the TV set.

"Great! The Rangers scored a goal!" he declared in an excited tone. He looked at her with a question upon his

30

face, turned again to the TV, and then looked back to Kalinda. With raised brows and an expression as though a light bulb had just turned on in his head, Gavin was up to something. "I hope you don't mind, but," he started, in a voice really too nice for him, "could we change seats? I'd like to keep an eye on the game."

He finished his request with that cute, overgrown-boy look, but it didn't work this time. Kalinda glared at him, the blood rushing to her cheeks. And all this time I was worried that he might try to make a pass at me—how ridiculous of me! Dealing with this guy was not going to be an easy task, even though she only had to put up with him for a short time. She could almost hear Kate saying, "You have to turn things around, see the positive side of being with Gavin."

So, being the sport she was, she answered, "Of course not," and quickly stood up to exchange seats. Once settled again, she slid her drink over and took another sip. Maybe Kate was right, she thought, be nice to the big lug —he might be more receptive to my ideas for the luggage line.

Oh, good grief! Her cashmere turtleneck sweater was starting to itch. She had been so careful about her dress, no more V necks for Big Red. She stole a peek at him out of the corner of her eye. His eyes were fixed on the TV. She scratched her neck quickly and discreetly.

"Hot?" Startled by his question, Kalinda's eyes darted over at Gavin. He was looking at her with a devilish glint in his eyes.

"A little," she shot back with narrowed brown eyes, pushing her shoulder-length brown hair away from her face. She moved her hand inside her collar, pretending to

31

straighten it, rolling it down and adjusting it, making certain it was even.

"Hello, Mr. Richards. The usual?" a short Irishman asked cheerfully. The waiter's timing was perfect!

"Yes, Michael. Kalinda, are you ready for another wine?" Gavin asked as he looked down at her half-empty glass.

"No, thank you," she returned politely.

With a nod of his head the little man was on his way to the bar.

Kalinda expected Gavin's eyes to return to the game, but they didn't. Instead, they seemed to want to dissect her. His eyes peered into her brown ones. His stare made Kalinda uneasy and she focused upon his large, folded hands across the table from her.

With keen interest he asked, "So what do you think of my choice?" Gavin gave a roving look across the room.

"Well, the place certainly has character, atmosphere," she offered readily, her voice trailing off at the end. She couldn't tell him she hated the place. Diplomacy was always the best policy, even though she felt like a traitor to her own sense of honesty.

He gave her a warm, wonderful smile, flashing white teeth. Perversely, Kalinda envisioned Gavin in his shorts with a little toothbrush in his big, masculine hand. Oh, God, Kate will die when she hears I was mentally undressing Big Red!

Gavin's head was cocked. "Knew you'd like it," he stated, very self-assured.

I didn't say I liked it, she thought sarcastically. "I can see why *you* like Damiens," she piped with an edge in her voice, tilting her head backward in the direction of the TV set. "How're they doing?"

32

"Fine. Just fine. Winning three to one." He seemed pleased that Kalinda was interested.

"Terrific," she said, her voice lacking enthusiasm.

An impish grin crossed his face. "I'm sorry I was rude. Unfortunately I'm hooked on hockey. . . . Married?"

His question came out of left field and Kalinda was taken aback. "No, I'm not," she replied slowly.

"I'm not either," he offered. "Recently divorced, that is."

Kalinda shook her head. "I'm sorry. Really. It must be very difficult for you." A flood of painful memories of her own divorce flashed through her mind.

"Sounds like you've been there too," he said with a gentleness that was comforting to see.

"Yes, I have. But I'd prefer not to talk about it."

"Still emotionally involved, I suppose," he persisted.

"No, not anymore." Kalinda sipped her wine, then added, "He's a wonderful person, but we weren't right for each other."

"Are you sure you're not still involved?"

"Gavin," Kalinda said sharply, suddenly disturbed by his probing questions, "we're here to talk about business, not my personal life."

The arrival of the waiter broke the tense moment. He placed what looked like a Scotch and soda in front of Gavin.

"Thanks, Michael," he said as he stirred the drink with a swizzle stick.

Gavin rested his head on the back of the booth, the muscles of his well-developed shoulders straining at the silk of his tailored shirt, and said in a low, intimate tone, "Still trying to hide behind that tough, business-lady facade?"

33

"Gavin, you're mistaken. I'm *not* hiding. We're here to discuss business, right? That's why, when you suggested dinner, I insisted upon lunch—because it's more businesslike. Less chance of a misunderstanding."

"I see," he said, but his expression was one more of curiosity than of understanding. Placing the swizzle stick in his mouth, Gavin turned the little rod between his lips and softly chewed on the end. His lips slightly puckered, his brow furrowed, and his head nodding, he seemed to be acknowledging something. He removed the swizzle stick from his mouth, placed it on the table, and raised his glass.

"Cheers," he said, and she raised her glass simultaneously to meet his. "To our working relationship," he said sarcastically.

"Thank you, Gavin," Kalinda returned with a forced smile. Intuitively she sensed the toast was no victory for her but a challenge from Gavin. "Do you have something against dealing with women in business?" she challenged.

"Seems like I've hit a nerve."

"Do you?" she repeated adamantly, refusing to be put off.

"What happened to the normal things women do, like getting married and having babies?"

"What if she isn't married, Gavin? What is she supposed to do, just hang around until—or I should say *in case*—Prince Charming rears his pretty head?" Kalinda hesitated and glanced down at the table, her index finger tracing the rim of the wineglass. She lifted her head and looked over at Gavin, her eyes serious. "Look, I'm not here to listen to you expound on a woman's role in the eighties. I'm here for one reason only—business, *my* business. If you have any problems working with me because

34

I'm a woman, let's hear them now. And stop all this personal chitchat," she said with controlled anger and determination in her voice.

"You don't beat around the bush, do you?"

"Well, I want us to settle this one way or the other. I want to know what your problem is about working women," Kalinda concluded, trying to figure out where Gavin was coming from. She was suddenly aware that she was relaxed now, confronting him this way. Her trepidations had melted away. And she was enjoying this direct conversation. Even if they didn't agree, at least they were being honest.

"In business," Gavin offered, "I think women are more manipulative, using their femininity, while men are more straightforward."

She thought about it for a moment then admitted she often felt the same way. "Sometimes they are more manipulative," Kalinda agreed, "but they have to be. They're survivors. If women have to use their femininity, it's because men like you won't deal with them on an equal basis. Usually a man will help another man because it's the ethical thing to do, but when a man helps a woman, it's often because he wants something, usually sex," she said pointedly.

"I suppose a lot of men come on to you," Gavin stated, truly concerned.

Kalinda nodded her head.

"That's a shame."

"Yes, it is, and it's a shame that other women go through it too."

Gavin shook his head. "I still can't picture you as this tough business type," he said softly.

"I know what I want and I'm not afraid to go after it.

35

If that's what you mean by tough, then I suggest, Gavin, you start picturing it, because that's exactly what I am."

"And this project is very important to you, isn't it, Kalinda?" Gavin asked, a mysterious quality in his voice, an intense look in his eyes.

"Yes, it is, Gavin . . . extremely so." Kalinda looked directly into his eyes. If he was going to suggest something, let him, she thought. She wasn't going to back down. His eyes were accentuated by a peculiar glint, and Kalinda would have given anything to know their meaning. But before she could ask him what he was thinking, someone caught his eye. A tall, very pretty woman with black hair stopped next to their table.

"Hello, Gavin," she said in a surprised yet happy tone. She bent over and gave him a kiss. Rising and turning to Kalinda, she said apologetically, "Excuse me for interrupting." Her voice was warm and friendly.

"That's all right," Kalinda replied, wondering who she was.

"Kalinda," Gavin piped in, "I'd like you to meet Carolyn." He was obviously glad to see the newcomer.

"It's nice to meet you, Carolyn," Kalinda said with a smile.

Carolyn smiled back. "Thank you. It's nice meeting you too," she said before returning to Gavin.

Kalinda had been conservative in her first impression of Carolyn. When her smile lit up her face, she was not just a pretty woman but a very beautiful one.

"I didn't know you were here, Gavin. I was just on my way to use the phone," Carolyn explained, indicating the archway behind him. "What have you been up to?" she added affectionately.

There was a certain awkwardness, a vulnerability,

about her that made Kalinda think Carolyn either had been or was intimate with Gavin. Strangely, Kalinda had never thought of Gavin as being involved with anyone. He certainly hadn't acted that way, and Kalinda suddenly found herself irritated with him because of the way he had come on to her.

"You know me, work, church, and home—that's my motto," Gavin teased and smiled over at Kalinda. She glared at him.

"How's everything with you, Carolyn?" Gavin asked sincerely.

"Fine," Carolyn said with a smile. She hesitated for a moment, looking down at the diamond ring on her left hand. Raising her hand and showing them the ring, she declared, "I just got engaged."

"It's beautiful," Kalinda said as soon as she saw the sparkling gem, and Gavin took Carolyn's hand and looked at the ring, giving an appreciative grin.

"I'm happy for you, Carolyn," he said, squeezing her hand gently before releasing it.

"Thanks, Gavin. I knew you would be." Then including both of them, Carolyn said, "I'd better be going. Bye." They said their farewells and the shapely brunette turned and left.

Gavin swigged his drink. There was no expression on his face, but he was studying Kalinda, watching for her reaction. She gave him none, but her eyes caught the movement behind him. It was Carolyn.

"No luck. Nobody's home," she said with a laugh as she moved quickly past their table.

"She's very attractive," Kalinda posed as Gavin's eyes followed in her direction.

"Uh-huh, she is. We used to date, but it wasn't fair of me to waste her time."

Kalinda's eyes widened. "You didn't want to marry her?"

"I thought you said we'd keep this to business," he said with amusement, and Kalinda gave him a dirty look. He was right, though she wasn't going to admit that to him.

Gavin chuckled. "Your silence is deadly. You must be used to getting your own way. Look, Carolyn's a very special person, but I want to keep my relationships light," he said matter-of-factly, as though it was a statement that he repeated quite often.

"So you don't want any commitments," Kalinda uttered coolly, with a judgmental attitude. Then catching herself—after all, it was none of her business, she reasoned—she added, "But I guess it's understandable, just going through a divorce and all."

Her cover-up did little good and Gavin gave her a quizzical look. Kalinda was acting like an open book.

"Do you want a commitment, Kalinda? A commitment is a full-time job, and so is a career. You have to have your priorities. Otherwise you end up in a juggling act that can be very tiring."

"I disagree. I know it can work. And what makes you think I'm not involved already?" Kalinda voiced, attempting to put an end to this conversation. Abruptly, before Gavin could say anything, she picked up the laminated menu. "What do you say we order? I'm starving." Placing the menu in front of her, Kalinda didn't have to look at the big lug, nor could Gavin see the disturbed look on her face.

"The food is really good," she heard him say.

Looking down the menu, she read out loud, "Last Card Louie and Portsmouth Fat. You must be kidding!"

"They're great sandwiches."

Kalinda lowered the menu with a smile on her lips, but what did it matter—he was watching the hockey game. Yells, clapping, and cheers went up from the men, which was the last straw for Kalinda. She let go of the menu and it fell with a thud across the table, just missing his drink. The sudden movement startled Gavin and he turned to her with questioning eyes.

"I'm ready to order," she said demurely.

"Everything's good. Steaks are excellent. Order anything you want." Gavin had immediately taken charge and Kalinda's business sense was alerted.

"Correction," Kalinda said in a low, controlled tone.

"What?"

"You're *my* guest—order anything *you* like," she stated politely but firmly.

Gavin ran his hand through his hair and sighed deeply. "Oh, Kalinda, I can't do that."

"Why not? You *are* my client, Gavin."

"That sounds so cut and dry. You make it sound so official, so cold-blooded. I didn't want us to have the typical business relationship."

Oh, and just what did you have in mind? Kalinda wondered, totally confused by his hot-and-cold behavior. But feeling light-headed from the wine and the hot room, Kalinda made no attempt to question him. She finished her drink instead.

"I'd like another please," she said as Gavin signaled the waiter. The waiter, having a knack for appearing on cue, was standing next to them.

"Two more please, Michael," Gavin said, and Michael nodded and hurried away.

Kalinda's index finger pressed against her lower lip as Gavin turned the menu around to face him. It was professional etiquette for Kalinda to pay for the dinner and she was determined to do so. "But, Gavin, it's business," she insisted.

His eyes were staring down at the menu as though studying it, but Kalinda knew better. He, no doubt, had memorized it. She got the distinct impression that she'd emphasized their working relationship a bit too much and perhaps she'd better back off. Maybe he was the old-fashioned kind and felt it was his duty to pick up the check. It was refreshing, at least, to think of Gavin having manners. Still, she didn't like the idea of being obligated to him. It was very manipulative of him not to follow standard business procedure.

Michael had appeared quietly at their table and placed their drinks in front of them, disappearing before a thank-you could be said.

Kalinda tasted the cool wine as Gavin drank his Scotch. "Okay, you win this time," she conceded with a laugh, "but don't take it as a precedent."

He looked at her, his face a calm mask, but his eyes were throwing off another signal.

In a quiet tone he said, "If you get the job, then you can take me out to dinner to celebrate, but until that time I'll pick up all the checks. And there will be other times, Kalinda. If you want this job, we have a lot of work to do, and I don't want to meet in either your office or mine. I spend too much time in mine as it is."

The smile frozen on her face, Kalinda was still hearing his words, *"If you get the job . . ."* Was he challenging her? Well, step back, you big lug, and watch me take you on.

"Well, what do you say?" The sound of his deep voice broke into her thoughts.

Whether Kalinda liked his arrangement or not, Gavin offered her no choice, and now that he had thrown down the gauntlet, she was determined to see him eat every last morsel of the dinner she would pay for when she landed this account. She just prayed that the time working with him would pass quickly.

Kalinda forced herself back into the conversation and replied, "Agreed. But since I'm going to get the job, I suggest we talk about the luggage line."

The corners of his lips turned slightly upward, and Kalinda could tell a smirk was dying to be born. She also knew he liked her confidence.

"Okay. We've decided the fabric is canvas. It's very durable and perfect for what we want."

"What about color?" Kalinda asked enthusiastically, relieved they were finally getting to business.

"Khaki or olive green."

"What about the trim?"

"It'll be leather. When you want something, does a switch go on, turning you on automatic pilot?"

Disregarding his remark, Kalinda smiled sweetly and continued, "Light or dark?" She wasn't going to let an antagonistic comment stand in her way of getting the facts on the luggage line.

"Light. Blond or more natural looking."

"That sounds very nice. I'll have Kate check out some good tanning facilities."

"I can help with that, Kalinda. That is, if you get stuck," Gavin stated with a chuckle.

41

"What's so funny?" she asked, irritated at him for making fun of her.

"*You* being stuck."

"First you couldn't see me as the tough business type; now you can't see me needing any help. Make up your mind," Kalinda teased. Then, in a more serious tone, she added, "It's nice of you to offer the help, Gavin."

"Anytime," he replied softly, moving closer and resting his chin on the palm of his hand.

Kalinda automatically moved inward and rested her chin upon her hand, her brown eyes looking deeply into his blue ones.

"How about a trunk?" she asked in a low whisper, her eyes still holding his with a serious expression on her face.

Gavin sat straight up, his hand hitting the table. "A what?" he asked in a disbelieving tone.

"A trunk," she repeated with an irritable edge to her voice. Kalinda couldn't fathom such a reaction to a trunk! "Yes, Kate and I thought you might need a trunk. We have many different designs; I'd be happy to show you."

"A trunk. That's a good idea, Kalinda. Sure, I'd like to see your designs," Gavin replied. But there was no enthusiasm behind his words, only annoyance. "I forgot to tell you," he declared with a smile, quickly dropping his previous attitude, "we want the design to have a fifties look."

Kalinda beamed. "Oh, Gavin, that's great. I'm really fond of that style."

"Good," he said with a shake of his red head. "Now let's eat. I'm hungry."

"Okay, I'm going to have a steak. No Last Card Louie for me," she said happily, totally in charge of the situation and feeling positive about the future of her company with the Richards luggage line.

"It figures," he said lightly. "You're unbelievable, Kalinda. I've never met anyone like you before."

Kalinda looked at this redheaded fellow with penetrating blue eyes sitting across from her. "Is that good or bad?" she asked in a deeper, softer voice, and even to her ears it sounded a wee bit flirtatious. It's got to be the wine, she thought to herself.

Gavin didn't reply to her question. Instead a brilliant smile was painted across his face.

It was late, and the dinner had gone fairly well. Kalinda and Gavin made their way through Damiens, past the bar. A few stragglers still hung on at the bar, and the air was heavy with stale cigarette smoke.

Once out into the night air, Kalinda sobered up and a chill ran through her body. Gavin leaned over and, to her surprise, buttoned the top button of her cashmere coat and raised the collar around her neck.

"Thank you," Kalinda murmured as she stared into his crystal-clear blue eyes. His hands were resting upon the collar of her coat.

"How about a nightcap? I live just around the corner," he whispered, his warm breath flowing across her cool cheeks.

"I'm sorry, but I can't. I have to get home, have to get up early," Kalinda returned, taking a deep breath. She felt restless, tied in one spot, and was anxious to be on her way.

"What are you afraid of?"

"Nothing," she stated flatly, turning and looking down the street for a cab.

"What if you didn't have to get up early . . . would you have come?" Gavin posed in a husky tone, an intense look upon his face.

"No, I wouldn't," she said simply, offering no explanations. Nor did she feel she owed him any. Business was over and she'd fulfilled her part of the bargain. She'd met Gavin, discussed the luggage line, and now it was late, time to go home.

"Do you want me to take you home?" Gavin asked, moving closer to her.

"No, that's okay, Gavin. I can get a cab."

Releasing her collar, his hands slid down to her shoulders. His fingers kneaded the back of her shoulders, and feeling their strength, Kalinda tensed. Bending down, he brought her closer to him and Kalinda closed her eyes, expecting the worst to happen and not knowing how she could get out of it. Big Red was finally going to make the big move! But instead, his warm, soft lips grazed her forehead with a kiss. Gavin had a way of getting under her skin by doing the opposite of what she expected, and his tender gesture made her uneasy, throwing her emotions into turmoil. Not wanting him to see her face, afraid of its being an open book, she turned her head toward the street. A speeding cab caught her eye.

"There's one!" she cried, indicating the cab.

Gavin released his hold and they dashed out into the street to wave it down.

Kalinda, light on her feet, took off like a bandit and reached the cab first. Her hand grabbed the handle of the car door as a larger one came down upon hers.

"Allow me," Gavin's deep voice insisted.

I can open my own doors! she wanted to scream at him, but she bit her tongue, letting go of the handle.

44

Gavin opened the door and Kalinda quickly slid inside.

Holding the door for her, he stated, "I'll be seeing you soon, Kalinda."

That sounded like a threat, Kalinda chuckled to herself, but she smiled and replied politely, "Thank you, Gavin," as he closed the door.

"Eighty-second and East End, please," Kalinda announced to the driver.

The cab started up First Avenue as Gavin waited and watched the taillights fading in the distance. But Kalinda didn't notice, her thoughts on other things far away. In a few days she'd be at Grace's party, seeing her dear friend again, and then afterward all of her energies and concentration would be centered around the Alan Richards luggage line.

CHAPTER THREE

She stood quietly, alone, taking in the spectacle before her, her eyes reflecting the dazzle of colored lights.

Tinsel, popcorn balls, mistletoe, smell of pine, and the ring of laughter—Kalinda's face brightened with a smile. The room, as usual, reflected Grace Roland's warmth and charm, her superb talent for capturing the holiday spirit for her guests.

Many fond memories of time spent in the Roland home flashed through Kalinda's mind. She sighed softly, glad she'd accepted Grace's invitation.

"Some champagne, Miss Forrest?" were the words that broke the magic spell. Old Wilfred stood stiffly, head held proudly, grasping a large silver tray containing champagne-filled crystal glasses.

"When are you going to call me Kalinda, Wilfred?" Her brown eyes sparkled challengingly at Grace Roland's devoted butler.

"It's only proper, Miss Forrest." His bushy gray eyebrows rose and fell, underscoring each word. "Seems more like Christmas with you here again in Edgartown."

"Thank you, Wilfred, I'm glad to be back," Kalinda returned warmly.

Wilfred's normally stoic face softened slightly with a trace of a smile.

Kalinda had the sudden urge to kiss the dear old man, but didn't, afraid the affectionate gesture might make him uncomfortable. Instead, her lips turned upward and she returned his smile.

"I'll tell Mrs. Roland you're here if I see her before you do," he stated. "You certainly have matured into a proper young woman," he added with a huge grin.

Kalinda laughed and cried, "Oh, Wilfred, you're too much!"

Wilfred looked totally pleased with himself as he moved the tray closer to Kalinda. "Would you care for some champagne? I remember it used to be your favorite."

"You don't forget anything, do you, Wilfred?" she said affectionately as she selected one of the glasses.

Wilfred carefully stepped toward another guest, and Kalinda raised the bubbling drink to her lips, sipped it, and glanced around the room.

Where is she? Kalinda anxiously wondered, simultaneously tapping her three-inch heel. Her eyes searched the room thoroughly until, finally, her glance fell upon the familiar, elegant face. With age, Grace's resemblance to Katharine Hepburn was even more pronounced. Her hair was worn in the Gibson style, Hepburn's trademark. Funny, even as a child, Kalinda had silently wondered if her mother's friend had deliberately fashioned herself after the famous actress. Grace caught her eye and waved, quickly making her way to Kalinda's side.

"Kalinda, my dear, I'm so happy you decided to come! I've missed you so much," the petite woman declared, giving Kalinda a hug.

It had been six long years since Kalinda had seen Grace, their only contact being the many long-distance telephone calls, and now the frailness of this vital woman brought tears to her eyes. She blinked them away quickly, taking in a deep breath. A clean, soft, flowery fragrance filled her senses—lavender. The aroma that had been etched forever in her memory, since early childhood, as identifiable with Grace. And always in Kalinda's thoughts, Grace had been inseparable from her mother and father. So much so that after their tragic death in the crash of their Piper Cub, Kalinda could not allow herself to visit this woman. Grace had become a living reminder of her loss. Time and distance had been put between them until the healing process had eased the pain, and Kalinda could now be with this dear friend.

She held Grace a moment longer, composing herself. Breaking the embrace, she looked warmly into the silver-haired woman's face.

"Grace, I've missed you too!"

"Let me look at you," her friend returned with sparkling blue eyes, holding Kalinda at arm's length. Her eyes took in the expertly applied makeup on a fair complexion, traveled over her sleek brown, shoulder-length hair, and rested upon her black designer suit.

Raising her head, Grace stated with genuine appreciation, "You look beautiful! That velvet suit and your hair. What did you do to it?"

Kalinda smiled. Grace would have to mention her

48

hair! It had always been such a long, thick, unruly mass of curls, and, of course, she'd always gotten hundreds of compliments on it. But curls were out in the corporate world, and straight, sleek hair was in.

"I've had it straightened," Kalinda explained matter-of-factly, sipping her champagne.

"You definitely look more sophisticated, but I miss the curls. Oh, I'm so glad to see you. Merry Christmas, Kalinda!" Grace voiced as she hugged Kalinda again.

"And you too, Grace! I know talking on the phone over the years can't make up for us not seeing each other, but I couldn't come before. Not until now. After my parents' deaths . . . there were too many memories. I needed time." Kalinda looked quickly away from Grace and stared blankly out into the distance.

"Yes, I know," Grace murmured in an almost inaudible voice. Then she was silent. Of course this gentle woman understood better than anyone. Grace had been her mother's closest friend and Kalinda's mother-in-law.

"Have you seen James?" Grace finally said with forced cheerfulness.

Kalinda followed Grace's glance to the tall, blond, good-looking James and a very attractive woman. They were totally engrossed in each other, their eyes betraying a couple very much in love.

"Yes, and I've met Candice. I'm happy he found someone. She seems perfect for him," Kalinda stated, her voice full of affection for her ex-husband, who had become one of her closest friends.

"Kalinda, there's something I want to say to you," Grace said softly as she gently squeezed the dark-haired woman's hand. "I've never said this before, but it means a lot to me that you and James have remained such good friends. I know, we were all very disappointed when your marriage didn't work out. It was difficult for me and your parents to understand. But later I think we all realized that the two of you grew up just assuming that you'd be married. All of us did. But what we hadn't noticed was the spark was missing. And I had hoped you would find it. . . . Is there anyone special in your life now?" Grace asked.

Kalinda did not answer. She glanced down at her glass, not wanting Grace to read her darkened eyes.

And after a moment Grace continued, "I'm sorry, Kalinda. I want you to be happy too."

"I know you do, Grace," Kalinda said quickly, blinking back the wetness from her eyes. "It's just that there isn't . . . and I wish there were. And I'm probably a little envious that James has found someone, even though I really am very happy for him. It seems every time we talk he's just bubbling over about Candice."

"Kalinda, I know you'll find the man who'll ignite that spark. Just give it time, dear." Grace's lips smiled warmly, not betraying the misty film glazing her bright eyes.

"Oh, Grace, I'm so happy you convinced me to come. You know, I've been standing here remembering all the wonderful times spent in this room. It looks so beautiful. You've always been so terrific at decorating. Why don't you come and give me some pointers on my office?" Kalinda said with a little laugh in her voice, slightly embarrassed about her long absence, even though she now knew Grace understood.

"I'd love to. I was wondering when you'd ask me," Grace jested as her long, slender hand brushed a rebellious wisp of hair back up into her hairdo. "Is it going as well as it was when we last spoke?"

"Couldn't be better. We've gotten some very important clients," Kalinda stated proudly, taking a sip of champagne.

"That doesn't surprise me—I always knew you'd be a success!" Grace declared enthusiastically.

"Thanks to you, our company may be a success. You'll never know how important your introduction to Alan Richards was. It was the nicest thing you could have done, Grace, and Kate sends her love and thanks," Kalinda stated. And what an unbelievable woman, she added silently to herself. If only I had half her energy.

"Oh, Kalinda, I was only too glad to be of help. Now tell me all the details," Grace continued in her chipper voice while her keen eyes quickly scanned the room and then focused back on Kalinda.

"Okay," Kalinda laughed. One thing was certain, she was going to leave out any mention of Gavin. "Well, as you know, the meeting with Alan went very well and he wants to give us the job. Kate and I will be working on some samples in canvas, khaki or olive green, with leather trim. I think we might do our manufacturing in Italy. We're off and running."

"Well now, if I decorate your office, you'll have to give me some pointers on my shop."

Kalinda chuckled. "I don't think there's anything I can teach *you!*"

"We'll see," Grace challenged. "Have you seen Alan yet?"

"No, I haven't. He's here already?" Kalinda's eyes widened, pleased in anticipation of seeing him again.

"Yes, he is. Let me go look for him. I know he's anxious to see you. I'll be right back."

"Yes, ma'am," Kalinda teased with a mock salute.

Grace smiled, then turned and left, the rustle of taffeta going with her.

Kalinda watched the silver-haired woman's graceful form float among her guests. Finally she stopped at a very stylish-looking couple. It was Alan and, no doubt, his wife. There was that certain oneness about them that only comes from sharing a life together. Kalinda couldn't wait to see the famous designer again and to meet his wife.

A sound caught her attention—it was sleigh bells on a horse-drawn carriage! She turned and gazed out the large picture window facing the street. A light snow had started to fall, and a horse, a handsome chestnut urged on by his driver in a black topcoat, made its way slowly past the white picket fence of the colonial-style home.

It was hard to believe that it had been so long since Kalinda had visited Edgartown—the charming old whaling village with stately mansions and tree-lined streets, the picturesque harbor protected by Chappaquiddick Island, and the quaint shops and stores.

As Kalinda thought about how quickly the years had passed, she became mesmerized by the snowflakes, which had become thicker. A time forgotten came to mind. Most of her childhood, her parents had owned a home on Martha's Vineyard where they had spent their summers and most holidays. One particular Christmas, when she was ten, Kalinda had been invited to her girl friend Sally's party only a few homes away. There had been a heavy snow the night before, and little Kalinda was having a difficult time getting through it when a snowball hit

52

her in the back. Furious, she had turned around—it had been her introduction to James. As it turned out, James had been aiming at his invisible buddy and Kalinda had been delighted with his mischievous nature. After that they had become inseparable, spending all their summers and holidays together. Finally, they had married during her senior year in college.

Her lips turned downward, a frown formed on her face. Kalinda recalled one of the most painful days in her life—the day she had admitted to James she wasn't happy, that there was something missing in their marriage. To her surprise and relief he had admitted that he had been harboring the same feelings. They had mistakenly interpreted love as familiarity and shared interests. Yes, Grace was right—the spark had been missing.

"Excuse me." The words were followed by a tap on the shoulder that broke Kalinda's thoughts and made her turn around. She raised her eyes quickly into blue eyes peering down at her—it was Gavin!

"I'm sorry, I didn't mean to startle you. I just wanted to say hello," he said in his deep, masculine voice.

What is he doing here? Kalinda thought with dismay, disliking the fact that he had interrupted her thoughts. But she replied politely, "Hello, Gavin."

He smiled warmly, then a puzzled expression crossed his face. "You know, Kalinda, when I first saw you in Alan's office, you seemed so familiar to me. I could have sworn I saw you before. I didn't mention it then because I thought I was imagining things. But the other night at Damiens, I knew I'd met you . . . somewhere. I was going to say something but you took off so quickly when we were standing in the street, I didn't get a chance."

Even as he spoke, the blood rushed to her pale cheeks,

the memory of his gentle kiss coming back to haunt her. "You're mistaken, Gavin. I never met you before I saw you in Alan's office."

"Are you certain?" he persisted as he lurched closer to her.

"I can assure you I haven't, Gavin. I would have remembered you," Kalinda insisted, backing away from his large frame.

"I hope I can take that as a compliment." He gave her a wink.

Oh now, doesn't he think he's cute! she thought resignedly. "If you wish," she replied flippantly, amused at his little gesture.

He studied her, his blue eyes boring into hers, while she wondered what he would try next. Then after a moment Gavin said, "I see, you think I'm making all this up."

"You must have me confused with someone else, Gavin." Kalinda smiled sweetly, then sighed heavily and gave a roaming eye to the people around her, hoping the big lug would catch the hint that she wanted to be left alone.

"Well, I see," he said. He shifted his weight impatiently while Kalinda's eyes focused on his expensive silk tie, which was loose around his neck and slightly askew. His sharp eyes followed her stare. With his large hands he grasped the tie, tightening and straightening it.

Kalinda's eyes took in his large frame. He wore a well-designed suit but his heavier build seemed more suitable to casual wear. Her eyes automatically went back to his tie, now hanging properly around his neck. Realizing he had pulled it too tightly, Gavin slipped his index finger inside the back of the collar and with a sharp movement toward the front, loosened the tie.

"It's a little warm in here," he declared simply as he beamed his grin.

Kalinda smiled in spite of herself and wondered how she could gracefully excuse herself from this character. She had not come to the Roland home to be with Gavin or to meet anyone.

"Come here often?" Gavin asked with inquisitive eyes.

"Oh, that's cute!" Kalinda said with a laugh.

"I mean, Kalinda, do you visit Martha's Vineyard often?" Gavin clarified, flashing her his enigmatic smile, totally ignoring her indifference to him and taking her off guard.

She answered, "No . . . not recently, that is. I spent a lot of my childhood here."

It was too late—the words were out of her mouth. Gavin had weaseled some information out of her and she didn't like it, offering conversation when she wanted to escape.

"You're a very interesting woman, Kal. And there's a lot I don't know about you, but I'll have plenty of time to find out." His blue eyes were tinted with gray.

"My name is Kalinda, not Kal. And I'd—"

"But Kal is more friendly, more intimate," he interrupted. "I hope you don't mind, but I'd like to call you Kal."

That was the last straw! Kalinda was now irritated with him for keeping her there and with herself for not being able to break away. Yes, irritation was knotting the muscles in her back.

"Look, Gavin, please don't call me that. I hate nicknames. And would you mind—I'd like to be left alone!"

Kalinda hated being rude, but this character was just too much! He refused to take a hint.

"Really!" he declared, almost amused.

She looked at him with narrowed eyes, black as the queen of spades. "Really," Kalinda stated in a low, cool voice.

A hurt expression crossed his face, like that of a little puppy dog being scolded for something he didn't understand. "Sorry, I thought maybe you'd enjoy a little company. Just trying to be sociable," he said in a sincere voice. Kalinda couldn't tell whether or not he was putting her on, but regardless of that Kalinda was starting to feel embarrassed, not liking the way she'd tried to brush him off. After all, he really hadn't done anything, it was just that she wanted to be alone. It was a private occasion for her to be in Grace's home again, and she didn't want to have to deal with Gavin. But her attitude certainly wasn't very gracious.

"I'm sorry, Gavin," she offered, "it's just that I guess I'm feeling a bit edgy after the long drive up here."

"I understand. It can be a bit rough, especially if you miss the ferry like we did." His voice was soft and his eyes warm.

Kalinda smiled. Perhaps Gavin wasn't so bad after all.

"Did you see the sleigh?" he asked suddenly.

"Yes, I did. It was beautiful."

"I was wondering if . . ." His words faltered, faint crimson flashing across his cheeks. Was he going to ask her to go for a ride? What a great idea, but was it possible —he was shy!

"Yes, you were saying?" To her surprise her voice sounded too eager. She wrinkled her forehead, trying to feign a serious, concerned expression.

His blue eyes sparkled brilliantly. "I was just wondering if you happened to know who was winning the game?" he asked offhandedly.

"Oh no, not again. You must be kidding!" Her mouth dropped open in disbelief.

"No, I'm not. I'm quite serious." He glared down at her. The shrewd, calculating look that she'd originally seen returned. "Do you?"

"Now that's original!" Her eyes flickered dangerously. He had gotten her attention; the game was on. She smiled a little wryly before she added, "If you're talking about the Sun Bowl, I haven't the foggiest idea, nor do I care."

Gavin cocked his head as a grin spread across his face. "I'm impressed—a woman who knows football!"

Kalinda laughed. "Now, now, I wouldn't want you to get the wrong impression. I just happened to come across that tidbit, believe me, by accident." What was she doing —she was actually encouraging him!

"Can I at least get you some more champagne?" he offered as he glanced down at her glass.

"No, thank you, I'm fine," she said imploringly, hoping he'd understand she wished to be alone.

"Well, okay, excuse me." He paused for a moment. "I'll find out where I saw you before," he added with definition, then shrugged his broad shoulders. "See you later, Kal."

Kalinda frowned as she watched him saunter away. He certainly was a strange fellow, and of all the people in the world, she had to work with him. It had never entered her mind that he would be at Grace's party.

A buzz of conversation caught her attention, and she drew herself back to the party. The talk ranged from politics to how the townspeople could keep fast-food chains off the island. Kalinda participated until Grace gently touched her arm and took her aside. "I know you know Alan, but I'd like you to meet his wife, Laura," Grace said. The well-bred Alan, looking very dignified in his tuxedo, exchanged smiles with Kalinda. His wife, a beautiful blonde with a great tan, wore an exquisite green sequined gown.

"Hello, Laura, I'm so pleased to meet you," Kalinda exclaimed as she extended her hand.

Taking Kalinda's hand, Alan's wife returned, "Thank you, Kalinda. I've heard so many wonderful things about you. I'm glad we finally have the opportunity to meet." Her words were spoken in one of the most melodious feminine voices Kalinda had ever heard.

"On that I'll excuse myself," Grace stated quickly and a little too cheerfully. "I know you'll all have plenty to talk about." Her puritanical white ruffled blouse did nothing to tone down the devilish look in her baby blue eyes. She bowed her head gracefully and left.

"She's so excited about the luggage line—even more than me, which I didn't think was possible," Kalinda said affectionately of her friend, watching Grace's slim figure disappear.

"Yes, she is," Alan stated. "She loves you very much."

"I know," Kalinda said softly, suddenly reminded of all those years without seeing this wonderful woman.

"Well, Grace said we were to talk about the project. She wants to make sure you get all the help and information you need to do the best job," Laura piped in, as though sensing Kalinda's sadness and wanting to change the subject for her.

Kalinda's eyes twinkled their thanks to Alan's wife, instantly knowing she liked this woman. "So that's what

58

her disappearing act was all about," Kalinda said with a laugh as Alan and Laura joined in.

"Yes, she's great," Alan finally stated. "Has Gavin filled you in on all the details about the line?"

"What Alan is leading up to is, how your meeting went with big brother." Laura moved closer to her husband for his confirmation, lights reflecting off her sequined gown, bathing her in a glow.

"Our meeting?" Kalinda murmured.

"Yes, Laura is right," he said with a grin. "She knows how disappointed I am that I'm not working directly with you, that I can't."

"I'm disappointed you can't, too," Kalinda returned sincerely. You think I'm just saying that, Alan, to be polite, she added to herself. If you only knew the half of it! "The meeting went well with Gavin," she stated convincingly. "We went over the color, design, and fabric. Kate is already looking into manufacturing facilities in Italy."

Slipping his arm around his wife's waist, Alan said, "That sounds great, Kalinda. But of course, if you need any help, any suggestions, if Gavin can't be reached, you can always call me. And I meant what I said about giving you the edge over your competitors. I just know you're going to bring in the best samples." He looked at Kalinda supportively.

"Thank you, Alan. I can't wait to get back to the city and get the samples in production," Kalinda declared.

"Good, I'll be waiting to hear from you," Alan stated, looking pleased.

"You'll be the first one I'll call," Kalinda said with a laugh, "as soon as—"

"Hello again!" interrupted Gavin, suddenly appearing next to Alan.

Oh, good grief, not him again! Kalinda forced a smile and continued, "As I was saying, Alan, I'll call you as soon as I know the samples are being airfreighted." Then she turned to the large man standing next to Alan.

"Oh, Gavin," she said with a forced smile as Gavin grinned from ear to ear.

"Sorry to interrupt, Kalinda," Gavin started politely before draping a large arm over his brother. "Alan, do you know who's winning the game?"

Lifting the heavy arm off his shoulder, Alan said, "No, this is a cocktail party, not a well-decorated barroom." Then he added, almost indulgently, "And, Gavin, I'm happy to say, there isn't a TV in sight."

"I was afraid of that. Maybe, I can dig one up," he replied enthusiastically, looking around the room.

"What?" Alan asked in disbelief. "You really are a lunatic."

"Now, now, little brother, we mustn't air our dirty linen in public. Besides, Kalinda will get the wrong impression of me," he stated as he turned his sharp blue eyes toward her.

There was something about the way he had said her name, followed by his penetrating gaze, that made her uneasy, but under the circumstances, all she could do was fake another smile.

"Precisely," Alan was saying as he caught Kalinda's eye. "I'm trying to warn her."

"I think, Alan, she can take care of herself. As a matter of fact, I'm *certain* she can," Gavin retorted, his eyes still on Kalinda, measuring her up.

You bet I can, Big Red, just watch me, Kalinda silently

60

threatened. Her eyes twinkled devilishly. "The only way to handle a guy like you is to prop you up in front of a TV set!" Kalinda returned with a haughty laugh.

Her laughter infected the others until finally Laura blurted out, "Gavin, I think she's got your number!"

A seriousness crept over his face, highlighted by a wrinkled brow. "We'll see," he stated, too casually, and Kalinda intuitively detected an underlying challenge. Then, in a more arrogant tone, he added, "Now if you all don't mind, I'm going to find out about the game."

A weightiness miraculously left Kalinda. She raised the glass that had been like a dead weight in her hand to her lips. The chill had left the champagne and so had the bubbles, but she didn't mind. Gavin had left, and Kalinda was more relaxed. She quickly finished the drink and placed it on a tray next to her. She looked up and caught Laura studying her.

"You'll have to forgive him, Kalinda," Laura said kindly. "He's a sports addict of the worst kind and we can't help but tease him about it. I'm just lucky Alan isn't." She flashed Alan a radiant smile.

"As if I had a choice," Alan joked as he took his wife's hand. "I think we'd better be going. The snow is getting worse."

Laura glanced out the window and then back to her husband. "It's a shame to leave so early, but I guess you're right. Our children are with a baby-sitter," she explained to Kalinda.

"I'm so glad I got to see you again, Kalinda. And I'll be waiting for that call!" Alan said enthusiastically. He was so polite and so charming that Kalinda still found it difficult to believe that he was related to Gavin.

"You'll hear from me soon," Kalinda promised cheerfully, offering her hand, which he took before he and Laura walked away.

Kalinda was left alone, feeling slightly flushed by all the excitement and very happy to be in the Roland home again.

"Oh, by the way—" It was Gavin's deep voice! "I remember where I saw you," he continued as she looked up into his smiling face.

Kalinda's eyes grew larger and her brows rose. What now? He certainly had the persistence of a mosquito! "Where?" she finally managed in a flat voice.

"In a photograph," he replied simply but smugly.

"A photograph," she repeated. "What photograph?"

"The one Grace showed me."

Now why would Grace show Gavin a picture of me? Oh boy, what a terrific line! Kalinda thought, irritated. "Well, I'm so glad the puzzle's been solved," she returned lightly, and dismissed it with a wave of her slender hand. A moment later she regretted that she had treated him so flippantly. The icy glint in his eyes gave her the uneasy impression that she had gone too far. "Why didn't you tell me you knew Grace?" she asked with curiosity and a smile, hoping to dispel the coldness she felt.

"You never asked. Would it have made a difference?" he asked in a low, intimate tone.

He probably thinks he sounds sexy, Kalinda quipped to herself. God, I hope it isn't his best shot! "Probably not," she teased, but to herself she knew she meant it.

"That's what I thought." He nodded and a small grin graced his face. The expression was strangely refreshing.

"I was a bit rude," Kalinda admitted in a voice that almost convinced her of her sincerity.

"Does that have the ring of an apology?"

She forced a smile and replied, "Could be."

"Accepted," he agreed with a raised blond brow and a grin. "You know, I didn't realize that Grace was your ex-mother-in-law. I just didn't put two and two together." Kalinda glared at him. "When I asked you about your ex-husband the other night, I honestly didn't know," he continued, seemingly indifferent to her expression.

"What's this all about, Gavin?" Kalinda asked in a cool tone, her patience worn thin.

"James seems like a nice fellow. It's a shame it didn't work out, Kal," Gavin said softly.

"I told you not to call me that!" Kalinda flared. "And as far as my personal life is concerned, I suggest, Big Red, you butt out where—" Kalinda froze. It was too late—she'd slipped. Oh no, what have I done, Kalinda thought morosely, slapping her hand over her mouth.

To her surprise Gavin let out a loud roar. The big oaf found it funny! Is there no limit to this guy's immunity to insults! Kalinda thought, now angry.

"Big Red, huh? And from a lady who hates nicknames. Well, one never knows," Gavin declared in a gruff voice, clearly amused by her embarrassment. A peculiar expression settled upon his face as he stared at her for a moment. He looked her up and down, as though checking out her size, as if he were packing her into a crate and shipping her overseas. He glanced up to the ceiling, placing his hands on her shoulders, and looked back into her eyes, now peppered with curiosity.

"Would you mind moving this way a bit?" Gavin requested kindly, guiding her to his right. Kalinda frowned but conceded. He glanced up again. "No, no, over this way, just a little," he stated in a methodical tone as he moved her back a little to his left.

63

"But, Gavin, that's where I was before," Kalinda protested to indifferent ears. He was staring at the ceiling *again*. This time Kalinda's eyes followed his stare. Her lips parted slightly as her head tilted backward and her eyes caught sight of a green, weedy-looking plant dangling above her. Oh my God, it's mistletoe! she gasped to herself, but her discovery was too late. Gavin's lips swooped softly down upon her mouth, pressing her lips gently but firmly. His lips were warm and his kiss had a strong, overwhelming effect, so much so that Kalinda was too stunned to protest. Her breath came with difficulty and a tingling sensation teased the muscles in the back of her neck. Her lips yielded to his touch and Kalinda, unable to think clearly, was kissing him back. Gavin brought her closer to him, taking her in his arms. His chest muscles were taut and the sudden awareness of his virility snapped Kalinda back to her senses. Abruptly she broke his hold, pushing herself away from him.

"What the hell are you doing!" she hissed with indignation as she straightened her jacket and skirt, trying to minimize the awkwardness she was now feeling. Her emotions were jumbled. She had responded to his kiss. How was she going to bluff her way out of this one!

Gavin's eyes were bright. "And you thought I was only looking for a TV," he declared with a wicked laugh. "How's it feel to be kissed by *Big Red?*"

No one in her entire life had ever infuriated her so, and Kalinda blurted out, "Not bad, if you like being slobbered over by King Kong!"

Gavin chuckled softly. "From where I was standing, it sure seemed like you enjoyed it."

She felt as if she was standing there with egg on her face as she glared at him with darkened, narrowed eyes.

"I should have known manhandling was your style," Kalinda muttered in a low tone.

"Is that any way to talk to a client?" Gavin returned lightly, not bothered in the least by her sarcasm. "Anyway, have to go. Just wanted to give you a proper holiday good-bye. I'm sure I'll be seeing you . . . *soon.*"

She nodded politely, but thought wickedly, Not if I can help it. Her eyes watched his tall figure disappear, but this time Kalinda had a hard time dismissing Gavin from her mind, because no other man she knew would have dared to do what he had just pulled. And she was still feeling a bit shaky from the experience as she absent-mindedly traced the outline of her lips with the tip of her index finger. Kalinda had to forget about the incident, put out of her mind the memory of his kiss and the effect it had had upon her. She would concentrate on what a pleasure it was to be with her dear friend Grace again. She began thinking about her time with Grace and what they would do with the few days she had on the island. Probably after they'd brought each other up to date on what had been happening in their lives during the past six years, they would go shopping in Edgartown and Kalinda would spend time in Grace's store. These thoughts were comforting and her trepidations about Gavin were temporarily forgotten.

"Kalinda." She heard Grace's soft voice filtering through the maze. "Having a good time?"

"Wonderful!" Kalinda declared, happy to see her friend. "Oh, Grace, how can I ever thank you for inviting me here and for setting up the business appointment with Alan." Kalinda wrapped her arms affectionately around the little woman. Breaking the embrace, she looked intently into Grace's translucent eyes. "I never did ask you, how did you ever arrange it?"

Grace gave her a sly look, the message so clear that Kalinda couldn't miss it. The glint in her eyes was like a neon light flashing. "I thought you'd never ask! Well, the beginning of November," Grace began, "when I was in New York to see James—you remember, I called and our schedules conflicted." Kalinda nodded. "I had such little time. . . . Well, I had a talk with James and we discussed your business. Then I happened to have lunch with Laura, whose mother was a college classmate of mine, and with Gavin. They mentioned that Alan was looking for a company to manufacture a new line of luggage. And I thought, why not? So—"

"You suggested me!" Kalinda interrupted with a chuckle in her voice. "You're a foxy lady, you know that?"

"It's nice to know I haven't lost the touch," Grace admitted delightedly. Then in a more casual tone, too casual, she added, "What do you think of Gavin?"

"He's okay." The inquisitive look in Grace's eyes was a little too obvious. "Why?" Kalinda asked, her voice tinged with suspicion.

"He's a bachelor—recently divorced, that is." Grace's keen eyes watched for Kalinda's response.

Me and Gavin. How on earth did Grace come up with that combination, especially with her ability for matching elegance with style? "Yes, I know, he told me. I guess that eliminates him as a possible companion," Kalinda returned in a solemn voice, emphasizing each word. She wanted to make sure Grace knew that she did *not* share her enthusiasm for Gavin as a possible date—or anything else.

But to Kalinda's dismay her words seemed only to stimulate Grace's curiosity. She asked with revived interest, "Why do you say that?"

"A recently divorced man is to be avoided at all costs. Too many problems, too much guilt." Kalinda reflected on her own past experiences, and she cringed at the memory of them.

Grace stared at Kalinda for a moment, but her eyes were distant, as though she was weighing Kalinda's words. "Oh, I see, Kalinda," Grace finally said. "You mean not marriage material."

Kalinda nodded in agreement, and at the mention of marriage material Alan Richards came to mind. A half-smile formed on her lips. "I've never seen two brothers who were such opposites," Kalinda declared, thinking out loud.

Grace's eyebrows rose, a puzzled expression on her face. "You mean you find Alan and Gavin so different?" she asked.

Kalinda hadn't intended to voice her opinion and wasn't prepared for Grace's question. How could she say that she found one so well bred but uninteresting and the other often rude but exciting? How could she admit to Grace what she was afraid to admit to herself? Maybe a half-truth was better, at the moment, than trying to explain something that she really didn't understand herself.

"Grace, I know this sounds awful, but Alan is so much more dignified and polished than Gavin. Even in looks, Alan is striking and handsome while Gavin is . . . mediocre." Her voice trailed off at the end, the look in Grace's eyes telling her that her friend probably did think it unkind of her to say those things.

"Kalinda, I'm surprised that you're letting looks sway

you so much," Grace returned in a kind but disappointed voice.

"It's not just looks," Kalinda explained, "it's the behavior . . . the mannerisms." Kalinda shrugged her shoulders. There was no way she could make Grace understand. In Grace's eyes the two men were equal.

"Well, I think you're judging Gavin unfairly," Grace insisted. "At least, he was more complimentary toward you."

"What do you mean, Grace?" Her surprise echoed in her voice.

"Well, when I showed him your picture and told him about your business, he said he was impressed that you were not only attractive but intelligent too," Grace said, quite smug at repeating his comment.

"He told me you showed him a picture of me. Why did you do that?" Kalinda asked in a low voice, trying not to sound too curious.

"Well, I always carry one of you around with me and you know how proud I am of you, dear," Grace returned affectionately.

Gavin's words, that he'd seen her in a photograph, followed by his ridiculous smile, came to mind, disturbing her. "Grace, *when* did you show him my picture?" A sinking feeling darted through her as she remembered how cool and mistrustful she had been to Gavin.

"At the luncheon. Why?" Grace asked, somewhat distracted as she looked around the room.

Kalinda sighed heavily. "Oh, nothing. I just wondered," she replied in a weary voice, still feeling a slight twinge of guilt that she had treated him so flippantly. But then again, maybe he'd gotten what he deserved, Kalinda thought, suddenly recalling his sneaky kiss.

"Excuse me, darling," Grace said, unaware of her friend's dismay, "some friends are leaving. I'll be right back." She walked quickly to a group of people putting on their coats.

Darn! Remembering what she had said to him about his kiss made her cringe. It wasn't like her to be so rude to anyone. But then again, Gavin wasn't just anyone and if he hadn't been so sneaky in maneuvering her under that mistletoe, she reasoned . . . No, she wasn't being fair to him, she was only looking for excuses. The truth of the matter was, being in the Roland home again was a very special time for her and Gavin had intruded upon that feeling. He wasn't to blame. The timing had just been all wrong.

She would straighten it out with him. Her face brightened. After all, she would be working with him, for a while anyway. He would get to know her and see she wasn't usually rude—at least she hadn't been too bad with him at Damiens. It was just the circumstance. She would have handled this meeting differently. Kalinda felt a little better with the thought that she could correct her error. Besides, it would be in her best interest if they got along, especially if she was to become the Richards luggage licensee, Kalinda thought confidently.

But how she'd responded to his kiss was an entirely different matter. She'd be careful not to let *that* happen again. The kiss was to be forgotten and she would have to act as though it meant nothing to her. Better yet, she'd never mention it to Gavin. If she didn't bring it up, he'd have to know it didn't mean anything to her. That's it,

Kalinda thought with self-assurance, I'll just pretend it never happened.

Kalinda smiled broadly as she spotted Wilfred slowly making his way toward her with just the appropriate thing—a glass of champagne!

CHAPTER FOUR

"Gavin, what are *you* doing here!" Kalinda exclaimed, wide-eyed, standing with her coat on and a gym bag in her hand.

"I came to see you," Gavin returned simply, lounging up against the door of her office, blocking her exit.

Kalinda breathed deeply. He was the last person she wanted to see today, especially looking the way she did. It was her first day back at the office after her vacation and because it was a particularly slow time for business, they'd decided to have some much-needed repairs done in the office. Kalinda didn't have any appointments, and it was her day to go to the Sports Training Institute for a strenuous workout—part of her strict regime. So she'd dressed casually in a warm-up suit, hadn't bothered to put up her hair, and had worn very little makeup. She would have given anything to prevent Gavin from seeing her this way.

Dropping her bag to the floor, Kalinda threw up her

71

arms, totally frustrated. In a firm voice she said, "Don't you believe in making appointments?"

"I usually do but I thought I'd just drop by. Your receptionist let me in on her way out," he declared matter-of-factly.

"You're sure you didn't *slip* in when she was on her way out," Kalinda blasted back, galled by the audacity of this man. She studied him. Feeling warm, she opened the top two buttons on her coat. In truth, it was just like Linda to do something like that. She probably was in a hurry and let Gavin in, thinking he had an appointment. "I was on my way out," she mumbled, wishing for a magic potion to make him disappear.

"Guess you're not happy to see me, huh?" Gavin posed, looking into her brown eyes, breaking her thoughts.

Momentarily the disconcerting feeling subsided as she really studied him for the first time. His blue eyes stood out against his tanned face, accentuated by the rosy glow of winter still clinging to his cheeks, giving him a more healthy, handsome appearance. So the big guy had gotten away for a few days to soak up some sun, Kalinda thought sourly, vaguely jealous that he'd been somewhere warmer than Martha's Vineyard.

"I've missed you," he said softly, breaking the silence. The corners of his lips turned up slightly and a half-smile softened his serious expression.

When did you have time? she wanted to say, but her eyes were unwillingly riveted to his lips. Crimson brightened her cheeks as she was reminded of how easily she'd been taken over by his kiss. Worse yet, Gavin knew it too. Kalinda smiled and forced herself to act interested. "Your tan looks great. Been to Florida or the islands?"

72

"Florida. A friend of mine has a place down there. We'll have to go sometime," Gavin said in a very friendly way, too friendly for Kalinda's taste.

Ignoring his little innuendo, Kalinda replied, "Anyway, the sun agrees with you. A tan suits you well."

"Thanks, Kalinda. I think that's the first compliment you've ever given me."

"Don't let it go to your head!" she teased with a laugh.

Gavin leaned toward her. "Ah, don't spoil it. A little compliment won't tarnish your tough business image."

With raised brows and a lilt to her voice, Kalinda replied, "I wouldn't want you to change your opinion of *me.*" Then in a brisker tone, she added, "Speaking of business, why don't you take off your coat and have a seat." She indicated a chrome chair next to a white desk in her reception room.

"No, thanks," Gavin said simply, not offering any explanations.

"You are here on business, aren't you?" she asked, puzzled as to why else he would have appeared at her office.

"Actually I thought we'd go to lunch," Gavin stated enthusiastically, his eyes sparkling.

"Lunch?" Kalinda repeated, not believing what she heard. "I can't go to lunch!" she blurted out.

"Why not?" he asked with a cock of his head and a lopsided grin.

He's too much! Kalinda thought incredulously. "Because I wasn't going to lunch. Today's the day I work out at the gym," she explained, impatiently tapping her foot on the floor.

"You can go another day," he returned nonchalantly. Glancing down at her foot, he added, "Careful, you don't want to wear out the floor."

Kalinda's brow furrowed as she shot daggers at him. "I can't go another day, Gavin. I just got back from Grace's and I need to work out. Home-cooked meals put the weight on."

"You could use some weight," he stated, looking her up and down.

"I disagree," she returned bluntly, trying to think how she could get rid of him.

Glancing at his watch, he placed his hand on the doorknob and said, "Come on, we're late. I made a reservation." But Kalinda, glaring at him, didn't budge. "You want the job, don't you?" he asked, challenging her.

"Yes, but—"

"Well, we'd better get going," he interrupted. "They aren't going to hold our table forever. We have a lot of work to do if you're going to get that job."

"Gavin, what could lunch today possibly have to do with work?" Kalinda asked with an edge to her voice, thinking his offer of lunch sounded more like blackmail than anything else.

"We have lots of places to go. I want to look at some luggage. We can check out some designs—see if we can find something we both like."

"But I didn't bring any clothes for lunch," Kalinda said imploringly. "I'm dressed for the gym," she added as she unbuttoned her coat and opened it, showing him her velour suit. "I can't go like this."

"As a matter of fact I like you better this way," he said with a smile, seeming to enjoy her discomfort.

"Well, I don't feel so comfortable. What if one of my clients sees me looking this way," Kalinda argued. Gavin seemed to be thinking that over. Her brow rose skeptically, wondering if perhaps she'd made her point. Feeling he needed a little more convincing, she looked at him hopelessly. Maybe he would surrender to a woman in distress.

"I *am* a client," he insisted in a cute voice.

Kalinda's mouth dropped open. When she'd made that comment to him in Damiens about his being her client, she'd had a feeling he'd use it against her sooner or later.

"You'll have to give me a few minutes," she said flatly.

"Sure. When did you get back from Grace's?"

"New Year's Eve," Kalinda answered, puzzled as to why he had asked.

He looked at her with narrowed eyes. "I tried to call you but the line was busy. I thought we might bring in the new year together," he stated, smiling.

"Do you ever think of making dates in advance?" Kalinda quipped back.

"Did you have a good time?" he asked, ignoring her remark.

"Yes, Grace is always great to be with."

"I meant New Year's Eve," he said in a low tone.

Kalinda looked into his eyes, wondering if he was really serious. He must think I was with someone, she thought to herself with relish. He almost sounds jealous! No way was she going to let him know she had spent the evening alone with her phone out of order.

"Very relaxing," she murmured with a wicked glint in her eyes, pleased to be leading the big lug on.

"I see," he said coolly, with a raised brow and a downcast expression upon his face.

"I'll get ready," she said sweetly, triumphant that she had gotten to him. But her victory was short-lived. The click of heels told Kalinda that Kate was on her way out and a foreboding feeling fell over her.

"Kalinda, there you are. I thought you'd left," Kate said the moment she saw her. But she stopped short when she saw Gavin. "Oh, I'm sorry, I didn't know you were busy."

"This is Gavin Richards," Kalinda quickly explained. "Gavin, I'd like you to meet my partner and friend, Kate Greer."

They exchanged smiles as Kate offered her hand. Gavin shook it as Kate said warmly, "Hello, it's a pleasure to meet you." By the grin on Kate's face Kalinda knew her partner approved of him, and Kalinda thought the reaction a bit too obvious.

"I'm happy I finally got to meet you. I've heard such good things about you," Gavin returned pleasantly, releasing her hand.

"Kalinda's been known to exaggerate a bit when it comes to her friends," Kate said with a laugh, turning to Kalinda. "I'm glad you're still here. I went ahead and made an appointment to have a repairman come to your home tomorrow if that's all right with you," she explained. "I had to call about the office phones and I knew how anxious you were to get your phone fixed."

Kalinda frowned and shook her head slightly, hoping her friend would pick up on her signal not to say anything further about it.

"Kalinda's phone is out of order?" Gavin piped in to Kalinda's dismay.

"Yes, she had to spend New Year's Eve alone without a phone. Can you imagine that!" Kate blurted out.

Peering at Kalinda, a smirk danced across Gavin's face, and she could have died. "That must have been just *awful* for you, Kalinda," he said sarcastically.

"No, I enjoyed the quiet," Kalinda insisted stubbornly,

wishing to knock a few inches off the big guy. I wonder if the workmen fixing the shelving in my office would just happen to have a hammer in their toolbox, Kalinda thought with a murderous look in her eyes.

"Is tomorrow okay?" Kate inquired.

"Fine," Kalinda returned glumly.

"Why don't the two of you come into my office and make yourselves comfortable, instead of standing in this hallway," Kate offered congenially, not having an inkling of what was going on.

Still regarding Kalinda with an amused gleam in his eyes, Gavin returned, "Thanks, but we're going out."

"Excuse me," Kalinda said hastily, finding the hole to escape, "I have to get ready." She turned quickly and left, wondering if she could keep Gavin from dropping in on her again.

Kalinda sat opposite Gavin at a table in a very pleasant Italian restaurant finishing the last portion of linguine and white clam sauce, her favorite food. Usually when she was out with clients she only picked at her meals, preferring to concentrate on business. But today Gavin was leading her astray and she was enjoying it. Kalinda was even drinking wine, something she'd made a firm rule never to do during business hours. She yawned and could have easily curled up somewhere and gone to sleep.

"You look like a contented cat," Gavin said with a smile.

"I feel like one," Kalinda came back with a little laugh in her voice. "The food was terrific. But you're a bad influence on me, Gavin. I'm stuffed. Eating pasta and drinking wine and missing my exercise class. You're not helping my image any," Kalinda teased.

"At least I have some effect upon you," he said, giving her a meaningful look.

Kalinda smiled. Not the way you have in mind, she quipped to herself as she glanced at her watch. "We really must be going soon."

"Lots of work to do?"

"Yes, Gavin, I do have other clients."

Gavin leaned back in his chair, using his swizzle stick to poke at a book of matches sitting directly in front of him.

"You want to become a hockey player when you grow up?" Kalinda asked with amusement, and Gavin laughed.

"You're funny, you know that. Actually I was wondering if you'd thought about doing the manufacturing here in the States. I want you to get the job," he said with conviction.

Kalinda looked at him with keen interest. What had made him change his mind? In Damiens he had said *if* you get the job; now he said he wanted her to get it. Curious. "Well, we're checking into leather companies here, but we feel we'll do better in Italy for what we're looking for."

"I know of some good facilities here if you need them," he offered.

"Thanks, Gavin, but I think we can handle it."

"Okay, little lady." He dropped the swizzle stick on the table, glanced around the room, and then turned back to Kalinda. "Care for anything else?"

"I'm fine, thanks, Gavin." Kalinda took a sip of her wine and then asked, "What made you say you wanted me to get the job? That's nice of you, but it seems as if it's something you've thought over."

78

"You're lovely, Kalinda," Gavin said, changing the topic in his usual flip way. "I can't figure out why you haven't married again. I'd think some man would have grabbed you up."

"Guess I'm not going to get an answer to my question and guess I haven't met the right man."

"You haven't?" he posed. His words seemed to have a hidden meaning, given the way he raised his brows with an expectant look in his eyes. But Kalinda couldn't imagine what he was insinuating.

"No, I haven't," she repeated simply. Kalinda yawned again and quickly covered her mouth. "Excuse me," she said, slightly embarrassed.

"I hope it's not the company," he stated with a frown.

Kalinda laughed. "No, I'm sorry. It's just that I don't usually drink before evening."

"It seems like you don't indulge in a lot of things," he said in a seductive tone.

"What's that supposed to mean?" Kalinda snapped, not letting him get away with that one!

"It's just that I want to get to know you better, Kalinda."

"Why do you want to know me, Gavin?" A seriousness had crept into her voice and Kalinda hoped he hadn't detected the change.

"Because you're a lovely person and I also want you to know about me."

"Like what?"

"Well, that I enjoy a beautiful woman's company. I think life's great and you should make the most of it while you can."

"No involvements, no commitments. Is that what you

mean?" Even to Kalinda's ears her voice had an interrogating quality about it.

"Something like that," he replied with a nod of his head, indifferent to her tone. "I don't have anything against commitments, but everything has its place, its time."

"And you've just gone through a divorce."

"Yes, it was a very disastrous four years." His face darkened and he added, "I won't ever go through that again."

"I can understand why you feel that way, Gavin, but not all marriages are bad."

"Do you know one that's happy? What about your marriage? What happened?"

Kalinda glanced down at the table and wondered how she could talk about it after spending the last few years trying to block it out of her thoughts. She looked back up to him; his eyes were expectant, waiting for her answer. Odd, she thought, that she would even want to share it with Gavin, but somehow knowing that he had been through a similar experience made her less wary of him. "We were two different people, that's all," she said with a wave of her hand, trying to dismiss it lightly.

"Sometimes that's not bad, could be exciting. Opposites are supposed to attract, you know. Maybe you're a little too difficult to please," he said with a knowing look, followed by a wink.

"No, I'm not difficult to please," Kalinda shot back, annoyed at his childish behavior. "We cared about each other deeply, but something was missing. It didn't work."

"I still don't understand, Kalinda."

"Maybe it's better left unsaid—period," Kalinda stated, folding her hands on the table and stiffening her

80

back. I should have known better than to confide in you, she thought sourly.

"Are you involved with anyone now?" Gavin asked, not letting himself be put off.

"No, I'm not. What about you?" she ventured.

"No, I've made it very clear I don't have much to offer. What I went through in my marriage has taken its toll. But one thing I do know . . ." he started, then hesitated.

"What's that, Gavin?"

He placed his hand upon hers. "I want to spend more time with you." His blue eyes had such an intense quality about them, glazed with a vulnerable hue, that Kalinda found it very difficult to look into them. She stared down at his hands resting upon hers, wondering why he wanted to spend more time with her. He squeezed her hands firmly. She knew she should have withdrawn them, but didn't. His grip gave her a warm, comforting feeling, compelling her not to move them. The image of her sitting there in her blue velour warm-up suit, eating pasta and drinking wine during business hours, doing things she hadn't done in a long time, came to mind and a small smile threatened at the corners of her mouth. Being with Gavin was stimulating, yet very relaxing. Kalinda was feeling very good. She raised her eyes back to his.

"You are spending time with me," she said softly. "We have a business arrangement."

"Yes," he agreed. "And I told you I wanted you to get the job. But I'd like us to have something more personal."

"Why?" she asked calmly while a part of her became uneasy. She wasn't certain if she really wanted to know where this conversation was leading.

"Oh, for various reasons. I'm sure we could have a lot of fun together."

I bet you would like that, she thought to herself, suddenly very irritated. Abruptly pulling her hands away, she stated, "I don't know, Gavin. Most of my time is wrapped up in business."

Leaning back in his chair, Gavin sighed heavily. "Kalinda, you have everything a woman should have—looks, brains, success—and you're wasting it. You can't spend all of your time working. You won't get much enjoyment out of life that way."

"I'm enjoying myself," Kalinda returned defensively.

Gavin crossed his arms and rested them on the table, moving closer to Kalinda. "Well, you could be enjoying yourself a lot more," he insisted. "And that'll be my department. You work on the luggage line and I'll work on you."

Kalinda's dark eyebrows rose. "I don't know if I like the sound of that," she said very suspiciously.

Gavin grinned, acting very pleased with himself. "I meant, Kalinda, showing you another side of yourself that you've been denying, that's all. See, it wasn't as bad as it sounded."

"You seem to think you know me," Kalinda replied coolly.

"I think you're hiding, Kalinda. You should relax more, have fun, take chances. Let your hair down."

"Stop playing analyst, Gavin. I'm very happy with my life and I don't need you telling me otherwise," she responded, very much in control. "I think we'd better be going," she added, noticing the room had thinned out. "It's getting late."

"Okay, I'll get the check, but I hope you have your walking shoes on," he challenged.

" 'These *boots* were made for walking,' " Kalinda said with a laugh as she raised her leg, displaying a high-heeled, brown leather boot.

Gavin chuckled. "It looks like you're going stomping with those on."

Kalinda smiled, dropping her boot. "Maybe I'll do a little of that too," she replied, playfully tossing her head.

"I'd hoped you'd left them at Grace's house," he said casually, glancing down at her boots and then back to her. Kalinda's face reddened, remembering how rude she'd been to him at the party. He would have to bring that up!

"You certainly weren't *pussyfooting* around with that sneaky kiss of yours!" Kalinda flared, not wanting to explain that special time for her but instantly regretting her words. Speaking of cats, she'd just let one out of the bag, and the rosy glow on Gavin's cheeks told her he was delighted she had.

"Would you care for some coffee or dessert?" Kalinda looked up to see a tall, very attractive Italian waiter standing next to the table. Gavin glanced over at her with sparkling eyes as if asking her if she wanted anything.

"No, thank you," she murmured with downcast eyes as Gavin smiled at her.

He turned back to the waiter and replied, "Just the check, please."

As Kalinda watched him, her heart sank. She was becoming more attracted to Gavin and she didn't like it. They were in a business relationship and any kind of romance between them could cloud up the issues. The job with Alan Richards was too important to ruin with a casual fling. She would just have to find a way to spend less time with him.

Her office was white, decorated with white furniture trimmed with chrome and bamboo, and highlighted by two large corn plants. The room had an airy, tranquil feeling, reflecting Kalinda's concern for freedom and serenity.

It was eight fifteen in the morning and Kalinda sat at her desk, poring over photos of luggage from the fifties that Kate had gotten from the photograph division of the public library. But she couldn't concentrate; her mind kept wandering. She thought about her life and how far she'd come in the business world. Eight years ago she couldn't have imagined herself with a company. Seeing James and Candice in Grace's home had stirred up all kinds of feelings for Kalinda. It wasn't that she minded James's being with someone, because she was really very happy for him, but it made her think more about herself, her life, and how empty the hours sometimes were when she wasn't working. It had been six long years and Kalinda hadn't found anyone who excited her and made her want to spend the rest of her life with him. Perhaps she expected too much from a man. Kalinda shook her head. She wasn't the kind that could settle for less. Kate had always told her the right one would come along when she least expected him. Kalinda hoped her friend was right.

I must get back to work, Kalinda thought as she looked at the mess of papers on her desk. There were several messages that Gavin had called the day before when she was out with clients. The past few days he had a habit of popping into her office whenever the urge possessed him and calling with any excuse to talk about the luggage. She sighed heavily and put the messages aside, wondering how long she could put off calling him back.

Gavin. What a strange duck! He was difficult to figure out. He seemed to be a multifaceted man. He could be kind and affectionate, but also arrogant and chillingly indifferent. He also had a way of affecting her. No other man ever infuriated her so, made her feel like putty in his hands, yet gave her the sense of something exciting about to happen when she was around him. And Kalinda disliked him for being able to put her through all those changes. During the holiday week she had spent at Edgartown, Grace had discussed Gavin with Kalinda. Grace had said that Kalinda was only looking for excuses not to like him, that perhaps she was afraid of really getting involved with someone. At the time Kalinda had laughed, but Grace's words had nagged at her and now made her think. Perhaps it was possible. Her divorce had been extremely painful, especially considering that Grace and her parents were devastated by it and her parents never really understood why the marriage was dissolved. Kalinda had to admit this unresolved problem still haunted her, and talking with Grace had made it all the more clear to her.

The door to the outer office opened and closed, and Kalinda knew it was more than likely Kate. Her partner usually got to the office before nine. She was glad that Kate had arrived; she needed to talk with her about Gavin.

"Hi there," Kate said cheerfully, walking into Kalinda's office with a small brown bag in her hand, her face flushed by the cold air.

"Hi yourself," Kalinda returned lightly.

"You're up early this morning," Kate teased. She loved

needling Kalinda about how late she got to the office, which was early by most standards, since Kate had a knack of being the first one on the job.

"I have some coffee—want some?" Kate asked, setting the bag down on Kalinda's desk.

"Sure," Kalinda returned as she moved the photographs to make room for the cups.

Noticing the pictures, Kate declared, "See you were going over the photos. Like them?"

"Yes, they're terrific. I liked the lines. They certainly had style in those days. Working on this luggage line is going to be a lot of fun, Kate."

Kate nodded in agreement. "I have some sketches for you to look at. Oh, by the way, Big Red called a few more times after I talked with you yesterday," Kate stated, indicating the messages on Kalinda's desk.

"Yes, and I have to call him back." Kalinda frowned. "I'll wait until later," she added as Kate took out the coffee containers and began opening them. "Kate," Kalinda began tentatively, "I don't know if I'm the best person to handle the Richards account."

Kate studied her for a moment, her blue eyes becoming very serious, and then said earnestly, "I don't know why you're doubting yourself. You're the best person to do it, Kalinda."

"I don't know. Working with Gavin is getting a bit difficult. He wants to see me on a more personal basis and I'm getting uncomfortable."

Kate's black brows rose as her eyes adjusted to a sharper focus on Kalinda. "About his feelings or yours?"

Kalinda hesitated. Her friend knew her only too well. She felt awkward in admitting to Kate that she was getting involved with someone who was a client. Not that

86

her partner would really mind, but it was a professional taboo for Kalinda. With a self-conscious laugh, Kalinda said, "A little of both. I don't know what to do. I think I'm starting to like him a little too much, which I didn't think was possible, even though I'm trying not to. I don't want my feelings to interfere with our work. I'm afraid I might do something that could jeopardize our company."

"Kalinda, I know you'd never do that. Work is too important to you. Just relax, have fun."

Kalinda laughed. "That's what Gavin said—relax, have fun."

Kate nodded her head. "Well, I have to admit, I agree with him."

"Thanks," Kalinda returned with feigned hurt.

"Kalinda, we're going to get that account and you're going to get it for us," Kate stated, full of determination. "And I think you should show him the drawings I did, to see if we're on the right track."

"I suppose you're right," Kalinda replied reluctantly. "I guess that means you won't deal with him for me."

"Kalinda, there's no way we could change places now. Use the fact that he likes you. I know it sounds cold-blooded of me, but I think the big guy should get everything he deserves."

"And what if he ends up using me?" Kalinda asked, looking into her friend's eyes.

"Kalinda, that won't happen. It's really up to you what happens between the two of you."

"I'm not so sure about that, Kate. He doesn't want commitments. He's coming out of a divorce," Kalinda said, rubbing her hands across her cheeks. "Maybe I'm jumping the gun. The project should be over soon. I could be worrying for nothing. How about that coffee?"

Kate smiled and handed her a cup.

"Thanks. I'll call him later and set up an appointment for him to look at your sketches." Kalinda glanced at the papers on her desk as she took a sip of the coffee. "I've tons of people to get back to. I hope there aren't any problems, I have a lot of telexes to do."

"I'll get the sketches for you," Kate suggested quickly, picking up her coffee cup and moving toward the door.

Kalinda nodded as Kate disappeared. She rested her chin on her hands, folded on the desk in front of her, and sighed. Gavin—he certainly was beginning to complicate her life. He knew the relationship was short-term, so why was he coming on this strong to her? But then again, men always seemed to handle casual sex better than women did. It was only for a short time that she would be in contact with him, Kalinda reminded herself. It was only a short time—she was strong enough to hold out. She would not get involved with Gavin!

CHAPTER FIVE

Kalinda sat at her vanity mirror putting on the final touches of her makeup. Gavin would be picking her up at any minute. When she called him about the sketches, he sounded pleased, but then in a more excited voice he said he'd been calling her because he had a very special place he wanted to take her that evening. Even though it was last minute, Kalinda didn't have any reason to refuse. She didn't have any plans for the evening and quite frankly, she welcomed the idea of going out. Work had been extremely hectic and it would feel good to relax and unwind. Out of curiosity alone, Kalinda had said yes. Someplace special. She made a thorough search of her closet, looking for the right thing to wear. Finally she decided she couldn't wear anything less than her Alan Richards original, which she had saved—for something special! Why not? she had thought. After all, she could let him see she wasn't any slouch by surprising him with one of his brother's designs.

I wonder where he's taking me, Kalinda thought for

the hundredth time. Wouldn't it be funny if he were taking me to Lutèce, Kalinda mused with a wry grin. Not that going there was really important, but maybe Gavin had gotten the idea that she liked that type of elegant restaurant, she reasoned as she slipped a strand of pearls around her neck and fastened the clasp.

The buzzer rang and Kalinda jumped. She quickly checked her profile, making certain the makeup was blended in. The mixed gray and brown eye shadow highlighted her brown eyes well, making them appear larger and more alluring. Satisfied, Kalinda grabbed her blue beaded evening bag and moved out of the room toward the intercom. Reaching it, she pressed the button down and let Gavin know that she was on her way. As she passed her full-length mirror, Kalinda gave herself one last appraisal. The blue brocade gown with matching beaded jacket looked as if it had been made just for her and she couldn't help but smile at her reflection. "Not bad for a thirty-year-old lady," she declared with a haughty laugh. Taking her coat and slipping into it, she was out the door.

Gavin stood outside her brownstone with a cab waiting. "We have to hurry," he stated briskly the moment he spotted her.

That's a fine greeting, Kalinda quipped to herself, but feeling confident and excited, she ignored his lack of courtesy. "Hello, Gavin," she said pleasantly as she walked over to him. The cab door was open so Kalinda eased herself onto the seat and slid over to make room for him. He followed and as Kalinda watched him his trench coat opened and her eyes fell upon blue jeans. Blue jeans! she thought to herself as the shock registered. How on earth was he going to wear *blue jeans* to any fancy place!

What the hell could Gavin possibly have in store for her tonight? Had she been manipulated into something she'd dread? Why couldn't he have told me not to get too dressed! Kalinda thought, now starting to seethe over her embarrassment at being so overdressed compared to Gavin.

She blurted out, "Gavin, *where* are you taking me?"

"Relax. You'll have to wait and see. The traffic was backed up on the Drive. We're late," he grumbled, indifferent to her glaring eyes.

"I don't give a damn about the traffic! Why on earth didn't you tell me you were wearing jeans!"

"You didn't ask. Besides, where we're going anything's appropriate," he said simply but with a hint of amusement in his eyes.

His lackadaisical attitude and his amusement added fuel to the fire and Kalinda could have choked him right there. Fighting the impulse, she clasped her hands and rested them on her lap as her eyes darted away from him and focused on the tall buildings flashing by.

"Take this all the way down to Seventy-second and then cut over," Gavin instructed the cabdriver in his typically deep, masculine voice, and Kalinda mimicked it to herself with an antagonistic flair.

"Yeah, that's your best bet," the cabby grumbled, stepping on the gas as the cab moved quickly down East End Avenue.

Finally, not able to contain her silent rage any longer, Kalinda turned her fiery eyes back to him and flared, "Gavin, stop playing games! Answer me—*where* are you taking me?"

"A woman of fire. I like that. The color in your cheeks gives you a sexy glow." He seemed to be ignoring her inquisition until he added in a gentle but firm voice, "You'll have to wait, Kalinda. It'll be a real treat."

Kalinda glared at him. "I just bet," she mumbled, her exasperation wearing her down. *A treat,* she repeated silently. With Gavin's perverted sense of fun, that could mean anything! Kalinda gritted her teeth. There was nothing left for her to do but sit and wait.

The cab made a turn west and Kalinda still didn't have the faintest notion where they were going. The meter ticked away while Kalinda seethed. The cab went south for some time then crawled to a halt and Kalinda rolled down her window, wondering what was going on. A cold blast of air exploded across her face as she realized Madison Square Garden loomed above her. Cabs were arriving and departing, snarling up traffic. Another traffic jam, she thought with a frown. Gavin is going to be in a dither —what a shame!

"Just let us out anywhere along here," Gavin quickly instructed the driver.

He paid the fare, got out of his side of the cab, and came around to her side, opening the door while Kalinda tried to register what was happening. Gavin stood before her as she looked up hesitantly, her blinking eyes strained by the brightness of the lights surrounding the marquee. *Tonight! NHL Hockey!* it boasted.

"Come on," he urged, offering her his hand. "Sorry, we don't have time for dinner first, but maybe a little popcorn or a hot dog will suffice until we have dinner later," Gavin declared, helping Kalinda from the cab.

"A hot dog?" Kalinda couldn't believe her ears. "You must be kidding! I can't believe you're taking me to a hockey game—I don't even like hockey!" she snapped furiously.

92

"You don't?" he asked in a disbelieving way.

"No, I don't! And I'm not dressed for a hockey game! How could you do this to me? You said someplace special, and I certainly don't call a hockey game special!"

"Well," he said with a shrug of his shoulders as he glanced at his watch. "Let's not keep standing here—let's go in and discuss it."

"Gavin, there's nothing to discuss. I want to go home."

"Kalinda, you can't, they're great seats! Besides, that's not very businesslike of you," he taunted her, taking her arm. "Come on," he added in a softer voice, "you'll have fun."

Kalinda studied him. He was smiling, even though he was obviously anxious to make his way into the Garden. If only she could get a deadly grip around his neck. But as a practical matter, Kalinda decided, one dead client on her hands would definitely not be good for business. So what was left for her to do? She was already there and Gavin was right—her professional etiquette required her to stay and keep the client happy. God, was she getting sick and tired of the word *professional!* It was becoming a noose around her neck. Well, she hadn't been to a hockey game in ages. . . . Maybe she could enjoy herself. But she'd feel like a real idiot being so fashionably dressed. Who'd wear an Alan Richards original to a hockey game!

"Come on, Kalinda," Gavin repeated, bringing her closer to him. His breath steamed out against the cold night air and Kalinda shuddered, the chill permeating her body.

She nodded helplessly and said, "Okay, but I want you to know it's only because I believe in doing the right

93

thing. You should have told me you were bringing me here."

"And ruin my surprise?" he gasped with an impish grin. Kalinda started to set him straight, but he took her hand and led her toward the arena. "Walk faster, Kalinda, we have to hurry."

Off they went, Kalinda half-running to keep up with Gavin's quick stride. Kate would be proud of me, she thought feebly as she allowed herself to be dragged to the game.

The national anthem had just ended as Kalinda and Gavin made their way into the arena. Once in their seats, Kalinda slipped out of her coat and gave a sly glance at the people around her, making certain that no one had noticed her gown and was pointing a finger at her. But Kalinda's concern was for naught; everyone's eyes were fixed upon the two players in the center of the rink as the referee dropped the puck. The slapping of their sticks rang out, and a roar went up from the fans around them, as a New York Ranger emerged with the puck. The lightning speed with which the players skated across the ice caught Kalinda's attention.

Even though she found the bone-crushing sound of the players slamming against the wallboards chilling, Kalinda was affected by the enthusiasm of the fans and she quickly became engrossed in the game. She ate popcorn and ice cream and even shared Gavin's beer, cheering the home team on like a real trooper. Gavin got a big kick out of her screaming, especially when Kalinda felt the referee had called one of the Rangers into the penalty box unjustly and yelled a profanity at him, making the couple in front of them turn around with glaring eyes. Gavin and Kalinda chuckled as Gavin wrapped his arm around her, giving her a big hug.

"You know, I haven't laughed so much in a long time," Kalinda finally said, looking into Gavin's blue eyes, her face reflecting a grateful expression.

"You're beautiful, Kalinda," he said softly. "I always want to see a smile on your face. If you play your cards right, I might always be around to put one there."

Kalinda sobered slightly. "Just watch the game, will you?"

Gavin turned his eyes back to the game and Kalinda was suddenly aware that she hadn't taken any time out in a long time to enjoy herself. Having a successful business meant long hours of hard work and little time for play.

Gavin reached over and took her hand, placing it on top of his jeans-clad thigh. He squeezed it gently and smiled at her before turning back to the game. Kalinda looked at her hand with Gavin's resting on top. Yes, tonight she was very attractive and elegant in her Richards original, but Kalinda envied the ease with which Gavin moved in his jeans. Then again, he was so much a man, it didn't matter what he wore.

Suddenly James came to mind. Her ex-husband would never have been caught dead in jeans—he was always so proper. He didn't approve of casual wear and believed Kalinda should follow his rule. Kalinda loved being casual and doing things on the spur of the moment, such as having friends over at the drop of a hat. But those things had made James uncomfortable and had put a strain on their marriage. Finally Kalinda had given up the struggle and become more careful with her dress and more formal with her friends. Even after she'd gotten into business, her ex-husband's critical eye seemed to haunt her and she

95

became more fastidious with her wardrobe, especially when meeting with clients. James would never think of going to a hockey game. The last one she'd attended was with her father when she was very young. But come to think of it, Kalinda admitted with a wry grin, most things James liked were very boring. Even their sexual life was unfulfilling, unexciting. Kalinda looked at Gavin slyly. I bet that wouldn't be the case with Big Red, she thought mischievously. Gavin turned and grinned, almost as though he had read her mind, and squeezed her hand.

Later that night Kalinda and Gavin dined in a small, intimate restaurant in Greenwich Village. Half-empty coffee cups sat before them on the candle-lit table. Kalinda stared into Gavin's eyes as the flames from the candle cast shadows across his face, creating ominous designs and playing havoc with his good looks. *Good looks* is it now, huh? Kalinda mused with a smile. The big lug is certainly growing on me!

"Private joke?" Gavin posed with a cock of his red head, catching her expression.

"You might say that," Kalinda returned smugly, silently refusing to let him in on it.

No reaction registered on his face as Gavin stared at her blankly, looking through her, not at her. He raised his cup to his lips and slowly drank the now cool coffee, placed it carefully back on the table, and gazed into the cup, obviously preoccupied with his thoughts. Studying him, Kalinda couldn't help but notice the few light, curly chest hairs that appeared at the top of his plaid shirt, like two desperadoes escaping their confines of jail for freedom. They reminded her of Gavin himself. He seemed to place his freedom above all else in his life—no ties for him. Kalinda couldn't allow herself to get caught up in her increasing attraction for him, to get close to him. It could mean only pain for her.

"Had a good time?" he suddenly asked, jerking Kalinda out of her thoughts.

"Yes, I did, Gavin. But hockey people are really crazy," she observed with a laugh.

Raising one light brow, Gavin gave her a skeptical glance. "Look who's talking."

Kalinda laughed, slightly embarrassed at being reminded of her behavior. "Guess I deserved that. I did get a bit carried away."

"A *bit?*" Gavin retorted with a chuckle, bringing a smile to her face. "But I admit I enjoyed every minute of your yelping," he said laughing again.

Kalinda screwed up her face and faked a scowl. "Yelping, huh? How cruel!" Kalinda retorted in her best venomous tone. The sparkle in Gavin's eyes cracked Kalinda's serious expression and she joined him in laughter. But as the mirthful moment quieted down, an awkward silence fell over them. A nerve jabbed ever so slightly above Gavin's jaw as he looked solemnly at Kalinda. What is he thinking? Kalinda wondered, tension exploding through her body, touched by his seductive eyes.

"How about an after-dinner cordial?" Gavin asked suddenly.

"Sure," Kalinda returned spontaneously.

"Cordon Bleu?"

"Fine. My favorite."

"We have a lot in common," he said warmly as he glanced over and signaled to the waiter. The man came

97

swiftly to the table and Gavin gave him his order. His eyes followed the waiter's departure, then turned abruptly back to Kalinda.

"You do my brother's design justice." Gavin threw an approving glance to the top of Kalinda's strapless dress.

Kalinda unconsciously rubbed her shoulder, bare since she'd removed the jacket earlier.

"I wondered if you'd noticed!" she said with a nervous laugh.

"Oh, I noticed all right," he admitted with a devilish glint in his eyes. "You know, I'm very attracted to you, Kalinda. I've made it very obvious."

Kalinda nodded, at a loss for anything better to do. Big Red was definitely making his move now and she hadn't responded with the annoyance she'd planned. She felt weak and confused, not certain of her emotions.

Almost in a whisper, Gavin said, "I want you, Kalinda. I want to make love to you."

But suddenly she was irritated. It was no longer just a compliment, it was a come-on!

"Why me?" Kalinda returned flippantly, letting him know she wouldn't fall for his line. "What about the rest of your girl friends?"

"There aren't any other girl friends, Kalinda," he responded in a quiet, sincere tone. "We could be good together. Why are you avoiding me?"

"Because you're not a very safe risk!"

It was ironic that she'd used the word safe, she thought mockingly. James had been safe and her marriage had been safe, but she hadn't been happy. There had been no excitement, no sparkle. Gavin may not be safe, but he certainly possessed the potential of adding pizazz to her life-style.

"I'm not James, if that's what you mean, Kalinda. And I don't think you want me to be. You're afraid to trust your feelings, but I'm a very patient man." His look of determination made Kalinda uneasy.

The waiter appeared quietly and placed the snifters of brandy before them without a word, as though sensing their serious mood, then continued about his business.

"We can help each other." Gavin seemed to be offering some kind of secret pact. The shadow of the flame suddenly flickered across his face, creating a villainous mask, and a horrible thought came to Kalinda's mind. Was Gavin insinuating she sleep with him for the job? Or was her mind only playing tricks on her?

Gavin raised his glass. "Cheers! To us," he toasted with inviting eyes.

Kalinda lifted her glass with a trembling hand, but her strong will came to the rescue. "To business!" she added with an overly pretentious enthusiasm, tapping his glass and beaming. If he thought for a minute she was going to be won over by a few lines of sweet talk, he was wrong. And if he had any funny ideas about a trade-off, sex for a luggage license, he had another think coming. Other clients had insinuated the same and she'd set them straight right away. And Gavin would be put in line too! But she wouldn't make accusations unless he pressed the issue.

"I have all the patience in the world—I can wait." Gavin challenged Kalinda with a broad grin, bringing the glass to his lips.

Kalinda smiled sweetly. Then you can wait until hell freezes over, she thought resolutely.

CHAPTER SIX

Kalinda sat at her telex machine finishing the last of the messages to be sent. Kate had gone to Italy to investigate the two factories they'd decided to choose between, so Kalinda was left to await her partner's decision, based on the factories' quality, pricing, and delivery dates. She was also left to run the business, which kept her more than busy.

Kalinda sighed heavily. Yes, their company had grown very rapidly this past year. The first year in business, they ran their company on a shoestring, operating out of a small, dingy room in a run-down building located in an out-of-the-way area. Their cash flow problem that year alone almost ruined their business. But their worst catastrophe came about the following year, when eight thousand handbags arrived poorly made. Stalling for time, they informed their client that the cartons had been lost in transit and went to their bank, managing by a hair to take out another loan to begin production of replacement bags. It was a tense couple of weeks for Kalinda and

Kate, but they presented their client with beautifully designed and manufactured bags. From then on, their company's success was on the rise.

Yes, their company had grown in leaps and bounds, and Kalinda would have given anything right now to have a few extra helping hands. There was so much to do, she didn't know what to do first. She glanced at her watch, shaking her head. Only a few hours left before she had to be at a client's office with the samples, but many hours of work lay ahead. The client was the marketing director of a very prestigious cosmetics company so she couldn't be late. Oh, now what? I still have to do the pricing, Kalinda suddenly remembered with knitted brows. She'd forgotten about it because it was a chore Kate always handled, but a necessary chore nonetheless. The price of success! Kalinda thought with a wry grin.

At least during the lull in the Richards project she'd managed to avoid Gavin. He had called a few times with invitations, but Kalinda had declined because of work and appointments with clients. Out of sight maybe, but not out of mind, Kalinda thought with a shake of her head. She thought of Gavin often, and whenever he came to mind, Kalinda did her best to concentrate on work instead. But he'd let her know he wanted her and he was willing to be patient. Why would he be so persistent in his pursuit of me, when I've made it clear this is only a business relationship? Do I represent a challenge to him? Kalinda was thoroughly perplexed. Well, she'd continue to put time and distance between them to allow her attraction for him to cool and hope that his attraction did the same. Her heavy work load had become her salvation.

Later that day Kalinda lugged two gigantic black bags across Fifty-seventh Street. She'd just left her client's office with a feeling of exultation. He'd been quite impressed with her presentation and had kept a few samples from which to choose the premium item to represent his company's fall promotion. But she'd walked several blocks with the heavy samples, trying to get a cab without any luck, and her elation was wearing thin fast. Kalinda paused at the curb, wondering which direction would provide her best bet for available cabs, when the honk of a horn startled her and made her turn around. A silver Mercedes pulled up alongside her, the passenger window gliding smoothly down. Kalinda automatically leaned over and peered in with squinty eyes. To her surprise Gavin sat behind the wheel with a Cheshire cat–like grin upon his face.

"Fancy meeting you!" Kalinda piped sarcastically, controlling her awkwardness at seeing him, irritated at the coincidence of his being in the same neighborhood as she and by how easily he penetrated her smooth veneer.

"Looks like you need some help," Gavin declared, giving her the once-over.

"No, I'm fine," Kalinda replied, feeling chilled to the bone and exhausted.

"Please get in," Gavin urged, reaching over and opening the door.

Kalinda hesitated for a moment. Of course it was ridiculous of her to stand out there and freeze, especially since she'd been trying to get a cab for at least fifteen minutes. The way she'd been avoiding him lately, she felt embarrassed to accept his offer, but more important, she didn't want to appear helpless. However, at this point her pride was the least of her worries. Her hands were starting to cramp from the weight of the bags and she was certain that frostbite was already at work on her toes. So Kalinda nodded politely and moved the bags toward the back seat.

"Hey, let me help you," Gavin offered, reaching toward the rear door.

"No, that's okay, I can manage," Kalinda insisted as she quickly opened the back door. With great effort and gritted teeth, Kalinda squeezed the bulky bags onto the classic blue leather seat. After closing the door she took a second to compose herself before sliding onto the seat next to him.

"Where to, little lady?" Gavin asked with a charming smile.

"To my office, big guy." Kalinda matched him with a saucy smile.

"Well, well—a woman with spirit," Gavin declared, stepping on the accelerator and directing the car away from the curb.

Kalinda glanced at him. His eyes were set straight ahead, his jaw was taut. A belligerent curl from his full head of well-groomed hair fell over his right eyebrow. And in her heart Kalinda knew she'd missed those sharp blue eyes, his ridiculous smile, and that mop of red hair. If only life could be simple. If she'd met Gavin at another time, in another place or situation, they might have had a chance at a relationship. He might have been over his divorce without the business deal looming between them. Who knows, it might have worked. But a lot of ifs don't make it possible, Kalinda thought wistfully as she turned her eyes toward the road before her.

"You've been a busy lady," Gavin said suddenly and Kalinda turned back to him.

"I've been *busy* with work, Gavin," Kalinda retorted

somewhat defensively, looking at his sharp-featured profile.

"I thought maybe you'd like to get away this weekend, spend some time in the mountains." His eyes turned to meet hers, gleaming with determination, before they focused back on the road. "We could have a good time," he tempted her, his voice carrying a soft, intimate quality. "Sit by a warm fire and—"

"Gavin, I can't," Kalinda interrupted. "I do have to work for a living."

"On the weekend? You'd be spending it with a client, if that makes you feel any better." His sarcasm was obvious.

"Gavin, I'm sick and tired of your throwing that client business in my face!" Kalinda flared.

"Okay, that was a low blow and I'm sorry. But isn't that what this is all about?" The car was stopped at a light and Gavin turned his intense eyes upon her. Their somber look made her uneasy.

"I don't jump into bed with just anyone," Kalinda reasoned in a voice that equaled the look in his eyes.

"Do you think I'm just anyone, Kalinda? I know you like me."

"You're pretty sure of yourself, aren't you?"

"A man knows these things about a woman," Gavin returned with a worldly air. The light changed and Kalinda was relieved that his eyes were focused ahead rather than on her. "I know you're attracted to me, Kalinda," he insisted. "I just don't know why you won't do anything about it. Being intimate with someone can be a very beautiful experience."

Kalinda was beginning to tire of this conversation. The

104

big lug was still talking about sex, not about liking her, and she wished she had just waited for a cab.

She glared at him. "I'm not looking simply for beautiful experiences, Gavin," she stated, exasperation scratching like sandpaper in her voice. "I want something more lasting."

"Kalinda, how do you know we can't have something lasting unless you give us a chance together?" He was right. But how did she know those weren't just words to get her into bed with him? No, Kalinda couldn't afford to be manipulated by him again, especially into an affair with him.

"Gavin, I'm sure you have plenty of friends to take to the mountains. I don't understand why you want me to go with you."

"I told you, I'm attracted to you. It's that simple."

"But Gavin, it isn't that simple. What do you have to offer?"

"Kalinda, what is that supposed to mean? Have to offer. At this point why is that important? Does every man have to offer you something before you'll have some fun?"

"You're missing the point. That's not what I meant." A silence fell over Kalinda as the car continued along its way. How could she tell him he wasn't just any man and that she could become deeply involved with him—could fall in love with him—and that she couldn't bear just a casual fling? How could she tell him that what she wanted him to offer her was a commitment, something he was unable to give. He was no longer someone just to push away; he had become very special to her. And because of these feelings for him it was becoming more and more difficult to resist his advances toward her, his ma-

105

nipulation of her into a sexual relationship. But why did he want her? Was it a trade-off, sex for love? If she were only a conquest to him, he might easily drop her cold after he'd conquered her, achieved his goal. And he'd already proved successful at manipulating her. God, she had to stay away from him! She didn't want or need any more pain in her life. She couldn't possibly be intimate with him. I cannot handle it! Kalinda insisted to herself with somber determination. Suddenly the ride seemed to last forever and she anxiously glanced out the window. To her relief they were approaching her office building.

"Guess we're here," Kalinda announced with forced cheerfulness. Gavin pulled the car over to the curb and turned off the ignition. "Thanks, Gavin," she said politely with a smile.

"Won't change your mind?" His blue eyes flickered persuasively.

"No, I won't, Gavin," Kalinda answered firmly as she opened the door and got out. "I can get the bags," she added quickly before closing the front door. Opening the rear door, she dragged the bags out, setting them on the sidewalk, then peered into the car with a forced smile upon her face.

"Hope you have a nice weekend. And thanks," Kalinda declared lightly. Gavin just nodded, his eyes slightly distant.

She carefully closed the door, picked up the heavy bags with apparent ease, and walked gingerly across the sidewalk and into the revolving doors. But once inside her office building she dropped the heavy weights with a sigh and pushed the button on the panel next to the elevator. As she waited, Gavin's words raced through her mind. A weekend in the mountains by a warm fire, huh? It sounded so enticing and delightful—too bad I can't risk going, Kalinda thought with a frown, tapping the heel of her boot. Thank God it's Thursday, she added silently, finding comfort in knowing she wouldn't be talking to him for a few days.

But what she'd admitted to herself just a few minutes ago in his car—that he'd become special to her, that she could love him and couldn't bear it if he broke her heart —came back to her. These thoughts would torment her, even when she and Gavin were apart. She had come to grips with her feelings only to realize she could never be with him. And she would wonder about his weekend in the mountains, Kalinda admitted with a sinking heart. The elevator doors suddenly opened. She lifted her bags and stepped in, her thoughts absorbed by this disquieting feeling.

CHAPTER SEVEN

Friday morning Kalinda stared at a telex from Kate. Her message stated she'd found that one of the factories was perfect for their manufacturing; the first samples were already in production and would be ready for approval in two weeks. *Just two more weeks,* Kalinda repeated over and over in her mind. The realization of the project's approaching completion filled her with a sense of confident expectation. Maybe they'd be extremely lucky and Alan would accept the first samples presented. Her contact with Gavin would lessen and her life would be back to normal again. She looked at the phone. She'd have to call Gavin and let him know about the samples. Then the weekend in the mountains came to mind. So what if Gavin would be going with someone else? He'd asked her and she had refused. With a shrug of her shoulders, Kalinda refused to dwell upon it. This was business and she did have to talk to him—period.

As Kalinda reached for the phone, it rang. Startled,

she said, "Hello," without even mentioning the company name.

"Kalinda, is that you?" The curious tone in his masculine voice made her laugh.

"Yes, it is, Gavin," Kalinda declared, "I was just about to call you."

"Great minds run on the same wave lengths," Gavin teased with a soft chuckle.

"I've got good news, Gavin—"

"You've decided to go away with me," Gavin guessed cheerfully, interrupting her.

"No, I haven't, Gavin! You certainly are a persistent devil!"

"But an adorable one." His voice was warm and inviting.

"I wanted to tell you about the samples," Kalinda explained, emphasizing her words so Gavin would understand she only had business on her mind. "They'll be arriving in two weeks," she continued. "So mark your calendar. Kate's decided upon a factory and she's very excited about it. Isn't that great news!" Kalinda waited for Gavin's response, but to her surprise there was silence at the other end of the line. "Gavin, are you there?"

"Well," he started, then stopped to clear his throat. "The reason I was calling was I made an appointment for us at a New Jersey factory that might be good to manufacture the luggage."

"But, Gavin—"

"Before you say anything, Kalinda, just listen to me. I'm not personally familiar with this factory but a very reliable business acquaintance of mine highly recommended it. He said the leather was top grade and the quality of their work excellent. I think we should see it."

"But, Gavin, I told you we could handle it."

"I know, Kalinda, but the factory is so close that if there are any problems with the production, you can go over there and correct it in an hour. It's not as if you have to wait weeks. I think you owe it to yourself and your company to take a look at it. That's why I went ahead and made an appointment for us to go over there and talk to the manager of the plant. He said he'd be happy to see us."

It was Kalinda's turn to be silent. Why on earth was he doing this to her? He was right—she should look at every option, and manufacturing in New Jersey did have its advantages—but damn it, he had no right to manipulate her like this! He'd made plans before without consulting her and he was doing it again, manipulating her and at the same time giving her a sound reason why she couldn't refuse what he was offering her.

"When are we supposed to go?" she asked grudgingly.

"This afternoon," he replied casually.

"This afternoon!" Kalinda let out a screech as she leaned against her desktop. "I can't go this afternoon!"

"I know it's last minute and I know I have a track record of doing this, but this time it wasn't my fault. Honest. I know you find that hard to believe, but the manager said this was one of the few days he had free for a while. I know how anxious you are for a good product and time is a crucial factor, so what could be better than to have your manufacturing done here and as quickly as possible."

"Okay, Gavin, you made your point," Kalinda relented. "I'd be a fool if I didn't go. But I've got two things to tell you. One, yes, you *are* doing what you call *this* again and I don't appreciate it, and two, I don't think

110

this little trip today is going to work out. Kate and I checked into a lot of factories around here and they didn't suit our needs. Most of them couldn't handle the quantity that we're talking about, nor could they meet a delivery of July or August."

"See you at one," Gavin instructed, ignoring her objections. Kalinda was instantly peeved.

"I guess I don't have much choice, do I?" she snapped without any pretense of her feelings. "I'll meet you downstairs, in front of my building."

"Fine. See you then. And, Kalinda, you won't regret going," he said reassuringly. "Bye."

"Good-bye."

Kalinda heard a click, followed by the silence of a dead line. She dropped the receiver on its cradle. Damn him! She now had two appointments to cancel! Her anger mounted and resentment burnt deep within her. She had to stop him from turning her days upside down on a minute's notice! Furthermore, she knew she was right about the factory. Kate and she had thoroughly researched all the local factories and hadn't found one that was adequate. So why on earth did he feel the need to drag her all the way out to New Jersey! Or was this his way of asserting his male dominance over her by undermining her business adeptness because she had rejected him and he had to salve his bruised ego? Good grief, she hoped she was wrong. Grief. I wonder if that's Big Red's middle name, Kalinda thought with annoyance. "Gavin Grief Richards—sounds right to me!" she said aloud with a wicked chuckle, flipping through her telephone file for her clients' numbers. Finding one she needed, Kalinda picked up the receiver to dial. At least it hadn't been boring with Gavin—that was the *only* positive thing she

111

could say about their relationship. But that was little consolation, considering she still had to deal with him this afternoon.

The setting was perfect for a romantic novel. The interior of a ship with its highly polished auburn wood paneling, brass-trimmed portholes, candle-lit hurricane lamps, soft piano music, and exquisite flower arrangements all blended seductively with the breathtaking view of Manhattan's glittering skyline across the Hudson River. But unfortunately the heroine's mood was out of sync with her surroundings—Kalinda was fuming.

They had arrived at the factory on time, only to wait an hour to meet the manager. Then within only a few minutes of talking with him, it was obvious that Kalinda had been right. The factory couldn't possibly meet the proposed deadline or the proposed quantities required for the luggage line. What's more, Gavin could have easily found out those details when talking to the man on the phone, instead of dragging her all the way out there and wasting her day. Afterward, he, of course, had apologized and offered to take her to an elegant restaurant for dinner. At that point her anger had almost paralyzed her and her polite business head had taken over and accepted his peace offering. But the charming atmosphere hadn't pulled her out of her rage. Instead it had just the opposite effect. The intimate backdrop only confirmed her suspicion that Gavin had once again manipulated her into being alone with him. Kalinda had spent most of her evening looking angrily across the water, wondering if Gavin was getting a big kick out of all this.

"Kalinda, you hardly touched your food and you've only said a few words all evening. What's the matter?"

Gavin asked as Kalinda turned to him and noted the concern in his eyes. "I told you, I'm sorry."

"I know you did, Gavin," Kalinda returned furiously. "But you undermined my business judgment. I told you that Kate and I had checked into all the local factories. You could have asked Mr. Green those basic questions over the phone. You didn't have to bring me out here and ruin my day. I'd like to know what the hell this wild-goose chase was all about?"

"You sound like a very suspicious lady."

"No, just a very angry one."

"Come on, Kalinda, you can't hold a grudge forever. Just look at this place. How can you still be angry with all this beauty around you?"

Kalinda grimaced, thinking how Gavin had resorted again to his evasion tactics! "You're right about that, but I'm not going to let you change the subject. I want to know what the hell this is all about!"

"Look, it was poor judgment on my part, but I didn't intentionally bring you out here to ruin your day. The factory came highly recommended and I knew you had to get your samples into production. But I do have to admit, I was motivated by the sheer fact that I wanted to see you. I didn't think there was any harm in setting up this appointment out of a selfish need on my part, especially if you might benefit from it. But you're right, I could have asked those questions over the phone. I just wasn't thinking clearly. Because when I think of you I can't think of anything else. I had hoped the factory would work out—you have to believe that, Kalinda. Forgive me? You have to forgive me," he pleaded softly, his lips sensuously alive.

Kalinda studied him for a moment. His eyes, tinged

113

with gray, held a vulnerable, open quality. Yes, she knew he brought her out there to see her and it annoyed her that he would use their business relationship that way. Why couldn't he just have been honest and told her that from the beginning? But she had to admit he had been honest in the end, confessing his wanting to be with her.

"How about it?" he asked, disrupting her thoughts. His voice sounded boyish and his eyes were imploring.

It's damn hard to stay mad at him, Kalinda conceded as a slight smile spread across her face. "You're incorrigible," she muttered. "Boy, when you make up your mind to get something, nothing stands in your way."

"I know—I want you," Gavin said in a quiet yet decisive tone. "You've been avoiding me, Kalinda, and it bothers me. Since we're being honest, I want to know why."

Kalinda turned away from his probing eyes and gazed out the window, directly in front of her, her eyes drinking in the shimmering water. How could she tell him that she'd been staying away from him because she knew she could really come to love him but didn't want to become involved with a man who couldn't return that commitment? She couldn't tell him that. He had made it very clear that he wanted no involvements and she wouldn't make herself vulnerable to him by revealing her feelings. She wouldn't throw herself at a man who couldn't love her back. Furthermore, what kind of man was he to manipulate her into being alone with him? She still hadn't totally gotten past her anger.

Bracing herself, she turned back to him and spoke with conviction, more to convince herself than anything else. "Gavin, I've tried to make it very clear to you. I want only a business relationship with you."

"Kalinda, what are you afraid of? You're a healthy woman with normal desires. What's the problem? I know you want me and you like being with me."

"Gavin, I don't want to discuss this any further," Kalinda said sharply, disliking the fact that Gavin could read her mind.

"Kalinda, I want you to understand some things about me. I'm not making any excuses, but I'm just coming out of a very painful divorce. And you know what the most painful part of it was?" Kalinda shook her head. "Marriage always meant forever to me. I married relatively late in life—in my midthirties. I waited because I wanted to make certain that I had enough money to support a wife and children. I came from a very poor family in The Bronx and I know how the lack of money can tear a family apart. And I also wanted to be certain of the woman I married. I wanted her to really love me and to share the rest of her life with me. I had everything planned out and I went into marriage positive that it would be perfect. I had a good job and I knew Elaine loved me. So what could go wrong? But it didn't work out the way it was supposed to. It wasn't very long before I realized the wonderful and loving woman I married didn't love me at all." Gavin hesitated as a pained expression crossed his face. Kalinda reached over sympathetically and touched his hand.

"You see, she was only interested in the Richards name and when the discussion of children came up, she always stalled, saying there'd be time. I finally had to admit she didn't want children and probably had never loved me. It was difficult. I loved her. At least I thought I did. Now I'm starting to question even that. Anyway, it was painful

115

being with her, knowing the truth. I'm not trying to bore you with my life story, Kalinda, but—"

"You're not boring me," Kalinda interrupted.

Gavin smiled appreciatively and took her hand in his. "Making a long story short, marriage took a lot out of me. And I'm not the same person I was then. I care for you, Kalinda, and I want to be with you. You're the first woman, since my divorce, I've wanted to spend time with. Why don't you give me a chance or at least think about it?"

Kalinda took a deep breath and exhaled slowly, calming her quivering nerves. She suddenly felt very close to Gavin and it gave her the disquieting feeling of entering a realm she'd never known. To be involved with him could mean a lot of heartbreak. But Gavin was looking at her, waiting for an answer, and she had to tell him something.

"I appreciate your telling me this. It was very personal and it does help me understand. I just need some time."

"Of course," Gavin returned in a low-pitched voice. "Would you care for more wine?" he asked, indicating her empty wineglass.

"No," Kalinda refused with a shake of her head and a light laugh. "I've had too much already. I'd love some coffee though."

"Great idea. Let me catch the waiter's eye." Gavin gently massaged Kalinda's hand before releasing it, anticipating a waiter. He glanced around the room, then something held his attention. Kalinda followed his stare. Couples, their bodies locked together, swayed to the beat of melodious piano music. She loved dancing and enjoyed watching the dancers' slow, rhythmic movements. One particular couple, who seemed well suited to one another and very much in love, caught her attention. The man had apparently said something funny, because the woman laughed and then affectionately placed her hands around his neck, bringing his lips down to hers, kissing him ardently. That simple, natural scene suddenly filled Kalinda with sadness and she envied how uncomplicated their relationship appeared. If only things could be simple, Kalinda thought, disheartened.

"How about a dance?" Gavin's words pulled her back to him. His eyes were focused keenly upon hers and he extended his hand. Kalinda smiled politely, slipping her hand into his as he gently eased her up and onto the dance floor. Wrapping his arm around her slender waist, Gavin drew Kalinda against his firm chest. His virility stirred her soft skin beneath the sheer fabric of her silk dress. His taut arm muscles teased her as she slid her hand up the outline of his jacket to the back of his neck. Just at that moment, the music stopped and the patrons applauded. Gavin lowered his head and a mischievous grin crossed his face.

"I wonder if that's an omen for us to stop too," he whispered warmly. His lips were only a heartbeat away from hers. Kalinda breathed in, but no oxygen reached her lungs. She had to put distance between them.

"Probably," she answered in a forced tone, taking her hand from around his neck and pressing it against his shoulder, trying to move away from him. But he held her tightly.

"Does it bother you, that you respond to me?" he asked softly, aware of her discomfort.

"I don't know what you're talking about," Kalinda protested with a contrary air.

"I'm talking about how your body came alive against mine, your breasts swelled at mere contact with my chest,

117

and now you're trying to run away. That's what I'm talking about."

Kalinda looked at him, a misty film clouding her eyes, and all words escaped her. He had zeroed in on the truth but she couldn't admit that to him. His lips brushed against hers lightly and then parted at the sound of the piano music. Gavin brought her close to him and they began to keep time with the melody. Once in his strong arms there was no ignoring the fact that Kalinda wanted to experience his magic. There could be no more denying her desires, needs—she wanted him. His strong body pressed next to hers and Kalinda knew she had to have him, at least once, at any cost. In spite of all the arguments, in spite of all the pain that might come, she would take this risk. She rested her head against his cheek, finally at peace with her decision, and drifted along with the music. It was one of Kalinda's favorite songs, "The Twelfth of Never," and she couldn't help humming the beautiful tune.

"Maybe you'll take a rain check on that weekend in the mountains," Gavin suggested somewhat confidently.

"Maybe," she murmured, too content to pay any attention to his presumptuous attitude.

"I've decided to take my two most favorite people this weekend," he revealed nonchalantly.

"Two!" Kalinda pulled away from him and looked up wild-eyed. To her indignation, Gavin let out a roar.

"What a picture you've painted of me!" But his voice sounded delighted, not annoyed. "My nephew and niece. I *am* an uncle, you know."

"Oh," Kalinda muttered dully, irritated with herself for responding so strongly.

"Well, don't sound so disappointed," he said with a

soft chuckle. "Come on, Kalinda, let's not waste this song. It's very appropriate for this evening, isn't it?" He looked at her intensely, his eyes projecting special meaning.

"It's a very beautiful song," Kalinda replied as they moved together and continued dancing.

Stalactite formations of melted wax accented the candles, the lights dimmed, the water sparkled, the music echoed, and Kalinda and Gavin danced on into the night.

Kalinda was curled up alone in her big double bed, her Icelandic down comforter pulled up to her chin. The clean aroma of his cologne still clung to her hands, a constant reminder of her desire for him.

She had spent a wonderful evening with Gavin, seeing a new side of him. His vulnerability had been revealed and now she understood him better. He was still carrying around a lot of pain from his marriage and really couldn't have a relationship with anyone. He had been honest and kind. And he'd made Kalinda feel that he cared for her. She'd finally decided, even if it was only once, she had to be with him. And no matter how much she might miss him after it, she would just have to handle it. She had enough faith in herself to know that she could. After all, as she had said to Gavin, she was a survivor.

Kalinda hoped sleep would come easily, but a gnawing feeling warned her otherwise. She was going on an adventure that could possibly affect the rest of her life. But she waited for the journey with a sense of excitement, regardless of the consequences.

The following Monday Kate returned from Italy with good news. Because the owner of the factory was anxious for their business, he had expedited production of the luggage samples and they were to be airfreighted ahead of schedule, on Wednesday. If they arrived by Friday, Kalinda could present Gavin and Alan with the samples on Monday. Kate and Kalinda were ecstatic about the news, especially about the prospect of having the design accepted and the project completed.

Kalinda called Gavin and he seemed pleased, but he added that he wanted to see her. She agreed, knowing that she had made a decision and sure that she could live with it.

They left work early on Thursday and drove to a country lodge in western Connecticut. It was a quaint, rustic inn surrounded on one side by a large iced-over pond and on the other by large pine trees and several small log cabins. The food and service were excellent. By the end of dinner Kalinda could no longer hide her attraction to Gavin. Feeling relaxed and confident, she admitted to him that she wanted to be alone with him. They decided to rent one of the cabins, but when Gavin turned the key in the lock Kalinda felt slightly awkward, like a vulnerable young woman making love for the first time. But she quickly shrugged off the feeling, not allowing anything to steer her from being with him.

Kalinda stretched out on the colorful patchwork quilt on the large canopy bed, watching Gavin place logs in the fireplace to start a fire. He had worn his white Aran sweater with jeans and looked very healthy, blending in well with the natural surroundings of the outdoors. Her eyes rested on the back of his head and she smiled wistfully to herself. Monday might be the presentation and after that, if the designs were accepted, she probably wouldn't be seeing much of Gavin, if she saw him at all.

It was what she had waited for and looked forward to, ever since she'd had to work with him. But now she was not experiencing the satisfaction she'd expected. Even though one part of her was relieved, he had grown on her and she would miss him.

"Warm enough?" he suddenly asked, turning around to her.

"Yes, I am," she murmured, studying the burning wood.

Gavin smiled and turned back to the fire. He stoked the logs again, and the flames darted, making a succession of slight, sharp, popping sounds. He placed the poker against the side of the fireplace and walked over to Kalinda's side, leaning over and giving her a warm, affectionate kiss. She looked into his eyes and knowing the time was right, she excused herself to the bathroom, needing a few moments alone to prepare herself for their lovemaking. With her mind and emotions united, Kalinda left the bathroom resolutely and returned to Gavin.

He was standing in front of the fireplace, gazing into the flames. She walked over to the bed, took off her robe, and slipped between the sheets. Gavin turned and looked at her, a serious hue glazing his brilliant blue eyes. He pulled off his sweater as he began to undress. Kalinda watched him, fascinated and then aroused at the sight of his truly beautiful body with its long, elegant lines, broad shoulders, smooth stomach, and muscular, but not muscle-bound, arms and legs. He walked over to the bed and gently pulled the sheet down and away, exposing her slender, well-proportioned body.

"You're so lovely!" he exclaimed with such an intense look of longing that her heart leapt to her throat.

He eased himself down next to her and took her in his

arms. She felt him shake slightly as their bodies met. His mouth found hers, kissing her gently. His tongue probed between her lips, searching deeper and deeper. He pressed against her and a tingle shot up her spine as she reached down and touched him.

"How I've wanted you," he moaned softly.

"Not like I've wanted you," she returned hoarsely, swept away by the thrill of his responsive body.

Making little circular movements with his tongue, he first kissed her neck, then traveled down her velvety skin toward her breasts. He cupped one ample breast in his large, masculine hand and brought his mouth over the soft, supple skin, his tongue teasing and manipulating the firm nipple. A sweet tension surged throughout her aching body, devouring her with the immediate need for him.

"Come, my darling," she cried with her hand placed upon his hip, trying to urge him over her.

"Don't you want to wait a little," he whispered in a deep, breathless voice.

"Gavin, I've waited long enough," she murmured as she guided his strong body over her waiting, anxious body. A soft cry rose from her throat as he entered her, his vitality filling her entire being. With their bodies entwined, he moved slowly, gently rocking back and forth, and then his movements became more erratic, building to a crescendo, his mouth pressed hard against hers. Their tensed bodies exploded together amid screams of joy and release. Gavin kissed her tenderly before moving off her and to her side. His breathing was uneven as he placed his head next to hers and she stroked his hair contentedly. Gavin suddenly emitted a low, soft chuckle, making her stir abruptly.

122

"What's so funny?" she demanded, wondering what had made him laugh.

"You," he said simply without any further explanation except a huge grin on his face.

"Me? You'd better explain yourself, or I'll wring your neck," she teased, placing her hands around his throat.

"Okay, okay, you win," he declared, taking her hands away from his neck and kissing them. "I was just wondering if 'Big Red' had lived up to your expectations," he declared with a wicked glint in his eyes.

"You devil! I *knew* you'd bring that up, I just didn't know *when!*"

"Just waiting for the opportune moment," he stated with great relish.

"I wondered what you were waiting for," Kalinda yelled, giving Gavin a big shove, nearly knocking him out of bed. His eyes widened in disbelief and Kalinda roared.

"So that's the way you want to play," he said, reaching over and pulling her roughly into his arms. "Tell me how you rate Big Red," he ordered in a frolicsome manner.

"Never," she refused defiantly with a spirited shake of her head. Kalinda struggled playfully as he brought his lips down upon hers, his fingers kneading the outline of her shoulders, moving down to her hip, and finally resting his hand on her stomach, massaging it ever so lightly. He released her lips, kissing her neck, and Kalinda wrapped her arms around his strong shoulders. Gavin inched down in the bed as his lips explored her breast and his hand slipped between her legs, touching her with careful, expert fingertips. Her fingernails grazed the smooth surface of his back as her body awakened, electrically charged by his touch. A moan escaped from Gavin's lips as Kalinda's body responded under his skillful guidance. She held him tightly to her and his body shook slightly as hers peaked to a frenzy.

"I want you now," she cried with an urgent, feverish desire to be close to him.

Gavin raised himself over her, his eyes vibrant and his cheeks flushed, and Kalinda was suddenly overwhelmed with such a feeling of vulnerability that she closed her eyes, wishing not to be seen. At that instant Kalinda knew she loved Gavin and had never felt this kind of love before and would never experience it again. At that moment she knew she was bound to him forever and when he left, a part of her would go with him. A tear threatened at the corner of her eye but was deadened by the sound of Gavin's voice.

"Look at me," he pleaded and Kalinda's eyes flew open. As his body arched above her, Gavin peered down at her with a strained expression on his face, as though he had sensed her pain.

"I see you. I see you, darling," Kalinda exclaimed as she pulled him down, close to her. He was hers for the moment, and she was going to live that moment.

"God how you excite me," he moaned and with one adept thrust, their bodies were locked together. The magic of his vital force filled her veins and rejuvenated her desire for him. Her stimulated body moved eagerly beneath his, and his responsive body quivered passionately. Their bodies met and were driven by an urgent, demanding furor. Time stood still as they gave themselves to each other, again and again. Their tumult continued to build as they were driven on by a mad fury to quench their insatiable appetite for each other. Finally the glistening bodies were still, like two prizefighters long past the tenth round and pushed way beyond their physical endurance. But the exhaustion was like sweet music to her soul. She was relaxed, at peace, complete.

Gavin reached over and took her hand in his. "I need you," he said softly.

Kalinda smiled, but thought sadly what a fool she'd been to think she could be satisfied with having him only once. But she had been right about her feelings for him. She loved him. And because she loved him, she'd let him go. Gavin, at this point in his life, had no intention of getting involved with her or anyone else. He was the type of man who needed space, room to make up his own mind, and her feelings of love for him would only be interpreted as a chain around his neck. Her love would only be felt as pressure and would scare him off. And Kalinda couldn't hide her feelings. For both their sakes Kalinda wouldn't allow herself to be alone with him ever again.

A chill swept through her body and Kalinda trembled. Oh, how she would miss him! The blood in her veins suddenly turned to ice and she doubted if she'd ever feel warm again. Now she would have to pay the price of knowing what it was like being with him and would miss sharing this wonderful intimacy because she couldn't compromise herself and settle for anything less than a commitment from him. So, she'd taken the risk and she'd lost.

Kalinda sat up. At a time like this she wished she smoked. In the movies the heroine always lit up a cigarette to get her through a difficult scene. She sighed deeply; she didn't have any crutches to get her through this one.

"Come here, you," Gavin declared as he pulled her back to him. "Where were you?"

125

"I was here." Kalinda smiled warmly.

"Are you sure?" He looked at her intensely, as though trying to read her mind. She nodded her head. "I'd thought you'd left me."

"Talk to me," she urged as she felt her eyes moisten.

"Want to know about my life?" he offered.

"Yes, I do, Gavin," she whispered, then laid her head against his chest to hide her face so he couldn't see the lonely tear that cried out her pain as it traveled down her cheek. Nor did she want him to know that being with him meant more to her than just having sex. No, she wouldn't let him see tears. She had enough pride in herself not to let him know how very special he'd become to her and how pained she was at knowing she wouldn't be with him again.

Kalinda curled quietly beside his warm body as he told her about his childhood. His Irish mother had died of complications resulting from his birth and his father married shortly after to provide his infant son with a home and mother. Alan was born a few years later at a time when his father was in great debt. His parents were consumed by constant fighting over money. So as soon as Gavin was able, he took on the responsibility of raising his younger brother. Very early Gavin recognized Alan's keen talent for design and worked long, hard hours to pay for the best fashion and design schooling available for his brother. Gavin also talked to Kalinda about his love for children, making her aware of how devoted he was to his brother's. Finally, both feeling very sleepy, they decided to stay over and drive back early in the morning. Without warning they fell into a deep, blissful sleep in each other's arms as the red hot embers of the fire slowly faded away into ashes.

126

Gavin stood on the steps of the brownstone where she lived, facing her. They had driven back early that Friday morning and Kalinda had to be dropped off at her home to change clothes before going to her office. A light snow was beginning to fall, dusting them with a white film as Gavin smiled down at her. He took her in his arms and kissed her lightly, then whispered warmly, "Am I going to see you tonight?"

Kalinda hesitated, her back stiffened, and then she uttered, "No, I don't think that's possible, Gavin."

"Why?"

"Because it's not possible, that's all."

Gavin's grip tightened on her arms. "Kalinda, that's not good enough. After what we've shared, you can't pull this. What are you doing?"

The pained expression in his eyes touched Kalinda and she knew the time was right to let him know how she felt about him. "All right, you want the truth. The truth is, I can't handle a relationship with a man who doesn't want me in his life permanently. It's that simple."

"But, Kalinda, I do care about you, you must know that!" he cried affectionately, giving her a hug.

But that's not enough for me, Kalinda thought, irritated that he hadn't dealt with the seriousness of her statement. "Gavin, I have to go," she said coolly as a shakiness overcame her body.

"Kalinda, don't go. Stay with me and let's talk about this," he pleaded.

"I can't, Gavin. I have too much work to do. The samples should be in today and I have to get ready. As you know, the presentation is Monday. Now that the project is just about over, I don't suppose we'll be seeing much of each other." Kalinda threw out those words in a last-ditch effort, hoping he would say something to make it possible for her to be with him again.

"Now that you've gotten what you wanted, you're giving me the deep freeze!" he accused in an icy tone and Kalinda instantly realized her well-intended words had been misinterpreted. But before she could say anything, he hissed, "That's the only thing that's important to you, isn't it, Kalinda—your work! Come to think of it, you and my ex-wife are just alike! You must have been cast from the same mold!" His blue eyes flared and a look of disdain crossed his face. Anything she might have said was totally blown away by his last accusation.

He turned sharply and strode away. Kalinda watched him as he got into his car and left, but she didn't feel anything—she was too numb. Then a queasy feeling jabbed at the pit of her stomach. How the hell could he have compared her to his wife! The woman who had given him so much pain and didn't want his children! God, didn't he know anything about her? Couldn't he tell from the way she'd responded to his body that she cared about him. She couldn't fake those feelings. And to love him would mean that she wanted to have his children. What a jerk! To think that she was *using* him, that she was only interested in him and slept with him as long as the luggage issue was on the line! And she had explained her feelings for him, but he had said nothing about that. What could he say when he had no intention of taking their relationship seriously, she reasoned. How could he possibly have thought those horrible things about her? Maybe he was just making excuses to get himself off the hook. But the look he'd given her had pierced through to her very soul and she wondered how long that disturbing image would haunt her.

CHAPTER EIGHT

Kalinda rested her head against the plush interior of the sleek black limousine as it traveled uptown and reflected upon the havoc of this morning's mad rush to prepare for the luggage presentation.

The magnificent samples had been delivered on Friday, but they'd arrived after working hours and after Kate had already left for an important business convention over the weekend. So everything had to be left until this morning, and Kalinda and Kate had worked very quickly, going over every aspect of their presentation. In their showroom Kalinda had rehearsed the order in which the individual pieces were to be shown, had memorized their prices, and had questioned Kate on every conceivable manufacturing detail that might be brought up. They had even rented a limousine to transport all their pieces of luggage over to the Richards office. But as they were ready to leave Kalinda and her partner had panicked. At the last minute they had realized that the light-colored leather trim should be protected but they didn't

129

have anything to cover the luggage. Frantically they had searched their office for something to use and had finally come up with, of all things, large black trash bags. After they'd carefully covered each piece, except for their handles, the chauffeur had made several trips back and forth from their office to the car, loading the luggage.

A small smile curled up the corners of Kalinda's lips. They were arriving at one of the most prestigious fashion companies with their samples covered by trash bags! Unthinkable and unheard-of! Thinking of how Kate had roared as she'd watched the chauffeur carry the large shiny containers down the hallway, she glanced over at her friend, who was sitting next to her with dull eyes focused straight ahead. Kate's a riot, Kalinda thought affectionately. With all of her bravado she's scared stiff that I might forget something and she'd have to get up and talk in front of Alan's panel of department heads and assistants. Talking in front of large groups of people was Kate's biggest dread in their business. She only went with Kalinda as a backup to provide any additional information about design or production that Kalinda might need.

Kalinda glanced at her watch. Two forty-five. Luckily the traffic wasn't bad and they were making good time. As they neared their destination, the images of Alan's and Gavin's faces came to mind. No wonder she had found it unbelievable that they were brothers. But after talking with Gavin it now made sense—they were stepbrothers. She'd hoped they'd be as excited and pleased with the samples as Kate and she had been. The only possible problem she could foresee was with Gavin, but Kalinda had to believe he wouldn't allow his personal feelings about her to interfere with his business judgment. She hadn't the heart to tell Kate about her misgivings regarding Gavin. She figured it would be better to wait until after the presentation to update Kate with her latest revelation about her relationship with him. That way if the samples were a success, Kate might not be as upset as she would be if Kalinda told her now.

As she glanced out the window she had to admit that she hoped he wouldn't be there today, particularly after their last meeting. Following his abrupt departure from her steps, the numbness had worn off and anger had snapped her back to reality. The fact that Kalinda had been vulnerable to him and he hadn't had the decency to acknowledge or deal with her feelings had pained her. Then to accuse her of using him and to compare her to his ex-wife outraged her. She'd have to make certain her eyes didn't trail off in Gavin's direction during her talk or she'd blow their whole deal because of the daggers in her darkened eyes. If only she'd listened to her mind, not her heart. It had warned her not to become involved with him, never to mix business with pleasure, and now she had to pay the price.

A sharp veer to the left shook Kalinda from her thoughts as the limousine pulled over to the curb next to the side entrance to 666 Fifth Avenue. The chauffeur switched off the ignition and the engine purred to a stop. Kalinda and Kate looked at each other but neither spoke. The moment was too important to allow their determination to be shaken by words colored by anxiety. The door opened on Kate's side and the two partners slid across the seat and out of the car. Silently they went about helping the chauffeur unload the luggage and then proceeded to remove the trash bags from the luggage before they were carried into the lobby of the building. Once into the elevator, Kalinda breathed easier. She glanced at her

131

watch. They were right on time. She smiled at Kate, her confidence returning. Kate gave her a look of relief, glad her partner had finally relaxed.

"We're going to knock 'em dead," Kalinda declared defiantly.

"They've got to love the luggage, Kalinda," Kate said with confidence, sounding like her old optimistic self.

Kalinda smiled in agreement as the elevator carried them up to their meeting. The gleaming doors opened at Alan's floor and Kate held the door as Kalinda took the luggage out of the elevator. Alan, who apparently had been summoned by the receptionist, appeared and helped them.

"Are you all set for your big moment?" Alan asked as the luggage was carried away by some men from his office.

"We're as ready as we'll ever be," Kalinda teased back, slightly out of breath and flushed. "Alan, I'd like you to meet the brains of the outfit, my partner Kate."

"Well put, Kalinda," Kate declared with a laugh and then in a more somber tone added, "I'm very pleased to meet you, Alan."

"The pleasure is all mine, Kate," Alan returned. "Well, I guess we'd better get started. The luggage has been taken into our boardroom. We've left one end of the table clear so you can present each piece. From what I've seen, you did a great job!"

"Thanks," Kate and Kalinda responded simultaneously.

Alan smiled with warm, friendly eyes and Kalinda knew he was truly impressed with their samples.

"Follow me." Alan led them past the reception area, through a red door, down the white corridor, beyond

132

several offices, and into a large, very masculine-looking room decorated with a long, narrow, thickly polished dark wood table surrounded, except at one end, by dark leather swivel chairs. On the wood-paneled walls hung Remington paintings. There were no windows but the room was well lit by antique lamps. The only softening effect was the two tall plants with their large glossy leaves situated at the end of the room. Their olive green luggage, trimmed in beige leather, had been placed on the floor next to the plants.

Alan's eyes quickly surveyed the room, before turning to the women. "Make yourselves comfortable. There's a closet behind that door," he stated, indicating a door to their left with a large wooden handle. "You'll be meeting my director of marketing, director of publicity, along with a few assistants et cetera. While the two of you get ready, I'll go around and round them up. How are you going to work this? Will the two of you be talking?" he asked with interested eyes.

"No, just me. Kate will help me with any additional information regarding the design or the manufacturing. She knows the intricacies of the design and the factory we'll be using," Kalinda explained as her eyes traveled back and forth between Alan and Kate. Her partner nodded in agreement.

"Fine. I'll be right back," Alan stated quickly and departed, closing the door behind him.

"Well, let's get busy," Kate stated as she noted Kalinda's preoccupation with her notes.

The two women removed their heavy winter coats and placed them, along with their personal items, in the closet. Then they systematically arranged the luggage. Kalinda rehearsed her presentation with Kate and only

133

for a fleeting moment did Gavin come to mind. Kalinda wondered why Alan hadn't mentioned his brother, but she dismissed him quickly. The future of her company was more important. It was also something that she had control over, and this was her opportunity to make the company a success. Gavin, on the other hand, she was convinced she couldn't affect in the least. Finally, her preparation complete, Kalinda checked her makeup for any last-minute repairs and retouched her lipstick. Satisfied with her appearance, Kalinda took her place, standing at the end of the table, with Kate sitting to her right, in the last chair on that side.

The door seemed to open almost on cue and Alan entered, leading a group of very distinguished-looking men wearing expertly tailored three-piece suits. Alan introduced them to Kalinda and Kate, and from their friendly attitudes Kalinda was certain Alan had talked to them about their company.

After the introductions were complete, a buzz of conversation overran the room. Kalinda looked anxiously over at Kate, who was talking to one of the men. Kalinda noted how beautiful she looked in her attractive blue dress and with her radiant smile. We're going to do it, Kate, Kalinda thought proudly to herself and patiently waited for the group to settle down. As a few moments passed, she felt butterflies in the pit of her stomach. All of the men had been seated and Kate also had taken a chair. Kalinda's eyes darted among the group, trying to determine which of the men would be the easiest to talk to or to have eye contact with during her presentation. But the task required little effort—the entire group seemed very open and receptive.

She then looked in Alan's direction. He was sitting at

the end of the table, directly opposite her. The chair on his left was empty. It probably had been reserved for Gavin. But the relief she'd thought she would feel at his absence was not forthcoming. Instead, she would have given anything to have seen the look on his face when their impressive luggage was shown. Yes, Kalinda felt cheated of her triumphant moment. Gavin might have denied her feelings but he *couldn't* deny her professionalism. Suddenly Alan caught her eye and with a warm smile and a dignified nod of his head gave her the go ahead to start the meeting. Kalinda smiled in acknowledgment.

She took a deep breath and began, "I would first like to say that my partner and I are very honored to be here today. Your company is one of the most respected fashion houses in the industry and—"

The sound of a doorknob turning, followed by the creak of a door, had caused eyes to shift from her to the door. Kalinda looked in the same direction to see who had caused the interruption. The red of his hair signaled immediately to her it was, no doubt, Gavin. What a rotten, lousy thing to do! How could he arrive late and interrupt her speech that way! He had gone too far this time!

"Excuse me," Gavin declared apologetically, seeming slightly uncomfortable over his intrusion, and closed the door quietly behind him.

"That's all right," Kalinda replied politely with a forced smile, while inside she steamed. How dare he interrupt her! It was the final straw! She clasped her hands to quiet her trembling rage. Her eyes trailed his movements as he walked over to the empty chair next to Alan. She waited as he sat, allowing herself the time needed to restore her composure. He looked up and their eyes met.

An irregular beat of her heart pounded in her chest. Gavin seemed different somehow. The keen, alert look to his eyes was gone. They were . . . duller, colder, or disinterested? But Kalinda couldn't allow herself the time or energy to figure it out. Nor could she allow him to manipulate her into flubbing her presentation because of his late entrance.

"Thank you. Please continue," Gavin suddenly stated, his voice flat and lifeless.

Her expressionless eyes lingered on him a moment longer before she slowly began again, her confidence returning. And as she talked, her anger subsided and was replaced by her natural enthusiasm for the samples.

Much of what happened in the remainder of the meeting was a blur in Kalinda's memory. She would have to rely upon Kate to fill her in on the details later. The only thing she was certain of was that the samples were a terrific success. Kalinda had definitely observed and remembered the obvious glint of appreciation in Gavin's eyes. But the first time she remembered breathing again was when she had rested her head in the limousine on her way back to the office with Kate.

Kalinda couldn't remember how long she had sat alone in the quiet of her office with only the dimly cast shadow of a fading sun and the phone cradled in the crook of her neck, the dial tone humming in her ear. Probably only a second had passed, but to Kalinda it seemed more like an eternity. Gently she replaced the bearer of good news on its hook, got up, and walked over to her window. She watched the multitude of ant-sized people on the sidewalk scampering home during rush hour. Their constant, determined efforts seemed so uncomplicated in such a complex life.

It had been less than an hour ago that she'd been in Alan's boardroom, and now hearing his positive answer had made her dream come true. But now, with the project that had been her focus completed, her feelings for Gavin immediately surfaced. And she admitted for the millionth time she loved him. She'd miss him, she thought sadly. But at least her involvement with him hadn't lasted long; maybe somehow that would help her throw her aching heart and soul into a new project. She desperately needed her work to distract her from the pain of its being over.

A light knocking on her door was heard, taking her away from her thoughts. She turned from her window and automatically switched on the light.

"Yes, come in," Kalinda called loudly and the door opened.

"What are you doing hibernating in here?" Kate said in her bubbly voice. "Linda said that a man just called and he sounded a lot like Alan Richards. What's up?" Her blue eyes were big as saucers.

Feeling ashamed of herself for not calling her friend in right away, Kalinda exclaimed, "Kate, I'm sorry. It *was* Alan and we *got* the job! I was just standing here, taking a few minutes, thinking about everything."

"Oh, Kalinda, I'm so happy! You did such a terrific sales job. How could we miss!" Kate declared happily.

"What about your designs! They did the selling themselves. He said the contract was being drawn up and it would be sent over by messenger at the end of the week. All we have to do is get the luggage in production and we're on our way."

"How about going out for some drinks to celebrate?" Kate suggested. "I want to hear everything he said."

"I'd love to, Kate. I just have to take care of a couple of things and I'll be set."

"Have you heard from Gavin?" Kate asked. Her voice had a more serious ring to it.

"No," Kalinda replied with downcast eyes.

"What's going on with you two?"

Kalinda didn't particularly want to discuss Gavin at the moment, but she could tell by the determined look in her partner's eyes there was no way to get around it.

"What do you mean?" she asked, still not wanting to offer any information.

Kate's brow wrinkled and she studied her friend for a moment. "He seemed to be waiting to talk to you after the meeting today and you just whizzed right past him."

"Did you see the way he sauntered in and interrupted me!" Kalinda proclaimed in her own defense.

"Maybe he had a good explanation and wanted to tell you," Kate offered, her voice softening. "Will you still be seeing so much of him . . . I mean, now that our samples have been accepted?"

A moist film suddenly clouded Kalinda's eyes at the thought of not seeing the big lug again. But she held back the tears and said in a quiet tone, "Can you imagine, I'm going to miss that guy. Remember all the trouble I gave you in the beginning because I didn't want to see him?"

"Kalinda, what's wrong? I don't understand."

"It's very simple, Kate, I've fallen in love with him and it's an impossible situation."

"Kalinda, that doesn't sound like you," Kate stated as she walked over to her friend. "Not from the woman who fought so hard to keep this company alive."

"Thanks, Kate," Kalinda said with a smile. "But that's something I can control. The affairs of someone else's heart are a different matter entirely. I told him how I felt," Kalinda said with a deep sigh and then walked over to her desk, sitting down.

Kate followed her and sat next to Kalinda. "And what did he say?"

"Nothing," Kalinda said simply and was touched by the concern she noted upon her friend's face.

"I can't believe that, Kalinda. He must have said something," Kate insisted with a glint of disbelief flickering in her eyes.

Kalinda shrugged her shoulders. "It was almost like he never heard me."

Kate's eyes brightened. "Maybe he didn't."

"Come on, Kate. You're really giving him the benefit of the doubt. That's not like you. Why?"

Kate raised her dark brows the way she always did when she was going to say something very important to her.

"Because, Kalinda, he's the first guy that you've really cared about. He's got to have a lot going for him. And I don't understand why you're giving up so easily. That's not like you. And I think you could be wrong about Gavin. What are you going to lose if you wait and give him a little more time? Things could work out, you know."

Kalinda was quiet for a moment, thinking over Kate's words. In a way her friend was right, but Gavin hadn't given her any reason to feel that he could be serious about her. Besides, she hadn't told Kate about his accusations.

Shaking her head, Kalinda stated, "No, I don't think

139

so. He's the type that needs his freedom. The last thing on earth he needs is for me to pressure him into a commitment. And I know at this point he would think I was forcing him into something he doesn't want. Besides, he said some pretty rotten things to me and I still haven't gotten over them." Kalinda's eyes darkened.

"Like what?"

"Like he thought I was using him to get the luggage deal and that I was like his ex-wife, who hurt him terribly."

"Oh, Kalinda, you have to talk to him. To say those things to you, he must be really hurting. And he must really care. You've got to straighten this out. At least talk to him," Kate pleaded, emphasizing her words with her expressive hands.

Kalinda stared at her friend, thinking how much she'd like to see Gavin. Then the look in his eyes the day he stood on her steps flashed through her mind and she thought about how he probably had intentionally set out to ruin her presentation by arriving late and throwing off her concentration.

"It's too late," she uttered, more to herself than to Kate.

"Kalinda, I don't believe—" Kate started, but was interrupted by the sound of the ringing phone.

Kalinda looked at the phone and then looked at Kate with a question written across her face.

Kate glanced at her watch. "Linda's probably already gone home."

Kalinda nodded and reached for the receiver.

"Hello, Bag Lab," she said.

"Hello, Kalinda. This is Laura. I hope I'm not catch-

140

ing you at the wrong time," Alan's wife said in her distinguished, melodious tone.

"No, not at all, Laura. I'm happy to hear from you," Kalinda said as she smiled over at Kate. Kate gave her one of her typical I-wonder-why-she's-calling looks.

"I hoped I'd catch you there. I wanted to congratulate you and to invite you and your partner to a party in your honor. What do you say?" Laura said in a voice that sounded very pleased with herself.

"A party. What a lovely idea! Kate and I would be happy to come, especially if it's in our honor," Kalinda said with a little laugh, her eyes catching Kate's excited expression.

"Good, I hope this Thursday isn't too short a notice?"

"No," Kalinda said, looking at Kate and deciding that her partner would break any possible plans she might have. "Thursday is fine," she added and Kate nodded.

"Many of our important buyers from some of the largest department stores throughout the country are in this week to attend the trade show at the Coliseum. Alan thought you should meet them, so I thought it would be a good idea to throw the party this week to celebrate and to allow you to meet some of your prospective clients," Laura said warmly.

"What a great idea, Laura. I don't know how to thank you."

"Just seeing you will be enough. I've already talked to Gavin and he'll be picking you up."

"He will?" Kalinda said, taken aback.

"I hope you don't mind my asking him." Laura responded immediately to the surprise in Kalinda's voice.

So he was asked to take me, Kalinda thought with mixed emotions of irritation and disappointment.

"No, that's fine," Kalinda replied quickly, not wanting to alert Laura to her falling-out with her brother-in-law.

"See you on Thursday then," Laura murmured before the two women exchanged good-byes.

Kalinda hung up the phone with a forlorn look upon her face.

"That's great!" Kate piped in cheerfully.

"No, it's not!" Kalinda returned adamantly.

"It's not?"

"Guess who's taking me to the party? I'll give you a hint—Laura asked *him.*"

"Gavin?" Kate said, giving her a disbelieving look.

"Yes, *Gavin's* taking me to the party," Kalinda confirmed with a look of annoyance. This had to be the worst piece of news she'd had in a long time, Kalinda thought miserably as she rested her chin on her folded hands.

CHAPTER NINE

The temperature was supposed to drop below freezing sometime later that night but Kalinda couldn't imagine it being any colder than the iciness in the air as she sat next to Gavin in his Mercedes. He had called her the day after she'd talked to Laura. Their conversation had been brief and civil, but they'd made the arrangements for Gavin to pick her up. She had not liked the idea of seeing him and had been tormented by that inevitability. She had been trapped into accepting his offer by a social obligation to Laura and Alan.

Gavin pulled his car in front of the Waldorf-Astoria and turned to Kalinda. "I must admit your samples were quite good. I never got a chance to tell you," he admitted in a gruff voice, disrupting their war of silence.

"I surprised you, didn't I?" Kalinda challenged with a sarcastic edge to her voice.

"No, I never underestimated your many talents," Gavin stated and gave her such a piercing gaze that Kalinda had to turn away. Limousines were unloading their

143

passengers in front of them and couples were hurrying into the warmth of the hotel. Why the hell did I get stuck with him? Kalinda hissed to herself. Social obligation or not, she wasn't going to sit here and take any guff from him! But she had to admit she was finding it difficult to cope with having to be with him again. She was going to do her best to bear up and not let him see how much she was hurting. She turned back to him with razor-sharp eyes.

"I don't know what you're insinuating, but it sounded like an insult to me. It wasn't my idea to be here with you tonight and I don't have to take your abuse. I've been abused enough," she blasted at him.

"We're here," Gavin said casually, as though not affected in the least by her words.

"Finally," she returned dully, but inside crumbling, knowing he was getting the better of her. But isn't that the way it is when one person cares and the other doesn't? she thought sarcastically to herself.

"Look, I'm only doing this as a favor to my sister-in-law," he stated coolly. "I don't want to be here any more than you do. So let's make the best of this and call a truce. What do you say?"

His words were like a dagger through her heart but Kalinda's face remained a composed mask of disdain. No way was she going to let him know how much she was hurting. A parking attendant had appeared at her side of the car and opened her door, anxiously awaiting her exit. Kalinda felt pressured into a prompt answer.

"Fine. A truce," Kalinda replied grudgingly, knowing it would be in her best interests to put up a good front with Gavin tonight.

Once out of the car, Kalinda's three-inch heels hit the

slippery sidewalk and Gavin was quickly at her side. "Allow me to offer my assistance to the damsel in distress," he offered with mock chivalry and gave her his arm.

"Over my dead body," she contended with a haughty shake of her head and took off over the treacherous concrete. But in her haste she'd forgotten about her long evening dress and took a giant step. The hem of her gown fell under her left foot. She shifted her weight immediately to her right, but the sudden movement caused her right heel to slide. Everything started to go into slow motion as Kalinda felt her legs slipping out from under her.

"Help me!" she screeched at Gavin, who had stationed himself alongside of her and was watching with an amused look upon his face.

"If you insist," he stated in a cocky tone as his arms tightened around her slender waist and Kalinda righted herself.

Finally, feeling securely planted, Kalinda removed his hands from her waist and snapped, "I could have fallen and you would have just stood there and watched!"

"I thought you had things under control," he replied smugly with his roguish smile.

"I just bet you did," Kalinda snarled at him, trying to dispel her momentary desire for him. *Damn* if he isn't good-looking, Kalinda admitted to herself with annoyance.

Without waiting for his response, Kalinda carefully inched herself across the sidewalk and over to the safety of the revolving door. Inside, she moved up the thickly carpeted, dark red stairs with a ginger gait, leaving the handsomely attired Gavin at her heels. At the top of the stairs Kalinda paused. The conspicuous bell-shaped

145

chandelier dangled above her as she stood on the mosaic medallion rug directly beneath it. Her eyes scanned the gold-trimmed room with its Art Deco walls until her eyes spotted the mirrored doors with the words Hilton Room inscribed on one side of them off to her right. It was where the party was being held, but Kalinda sped past it as she caught sight of the hatcheck room.

While she was removing her mink jacket, to her surprise Gavin's large hands came around its lapel and he said, "Allow me."

Kalinda didn't object, thinking it a congenial gesture on his part. He helped her out of her jacket and gave it, along with his overcoat, to the hatcheck woman in exchange for two claim checks. He handed a check to Kalinda.

Taking it, she replied in a polite tone, "Thank you, Gavin."

"Just wanted to make sure you arrived safe and sound," he returned indifferently, making her feel he would have extended this common courtesy to anyone.

Kalinda's temper flared again at the thought of how easily she'd been duped into agreeing to a peace treaty and how humiliating this all was for her. How impossible and arrogant he was. And how the hell was she going to get through this night? Kalinda frowned as she placed the check in her multicolored beaded evening bag and silently walked over to the entrance of the ballroom.

Gavin opened the glass door and Kalinda stepped into the elegantly decorated room. Two large chandeliers hung at each end of the rectangular shaped enclosure. Directly opposite her, a band on a raised platform surrounded by several floral bouquets played soft music.

"Kalinda!" was called in the familiar harmonic tone

and Kalinda looked over to see a vision of sequins and glitter as Alan's wife quickly made her way over to Kalinda's side.

"I thought the two of you would never get here," Laura exclaimed the moment she reached them. "I've already met Kate and she's terrific, Kalinda," she added with a smile.

"Thanks, Laura, I knew you'd like her. What a beautiful room. And all the people," Kalinda declared, noting the crowd milling around her. "I'm excited!"

"Well, there are lots of people for you to meet. Buyers from all over. Maybe Gavin should do the honors of escorting you around," Laura suggested, smiling up into Gavin's distant eyes.

"No, I think you should do it. You organized it all, Laura," Gavin declared decisively. He leaned over and kissed his sister-in-law's cheek and abruptly excused himself.

Laura was silent as she watched Gavin until his large frame finally disappeared amongst the cluster of people and turned back to Kalinda with worried eyes.

"I hope you don't mind my asking, but is there anything wrong? Did something happen between you two, or am I imagining things?" Laura asked with raised blond eyebrows and furrowed brow.

So it was apparent that Gavin had told Laura and Alan about their dating but hadn't informed them of their breakup. Kalinda felt uneasy about this discovery and didn't feel she knew Laura well enough to confide the truth. She decided that it was Gavin's place to tell them.

"Everything's fine," Kalinda answered casually, making certain her voice sounded natural, and gave Laura a sunny smile. "Gavin and I do have our differences though," she continued with a laugh.

Laura studied her for a moment, as though weighing Kalinda's words against her own woman's intuition. Her face brightened as if she had solved her dilemma.

"Okay, I'll accept that for now," Laura teased lightly, "that is, until I get my hands on my brother-in-law. Anyway, come on." Taking Kalinda's hand, Laura led her through the party and over to Kate.

Kate, of course, had immediately given her a look, signaling that she was anxious to know how Kalinda had made out with Gavin. Kalinda frowned, freezing Kate's expression cold, but too late, for Laura's keen eyes had already picked up on their exchange. Without remarking upon it, Laura swept the two women off, introducing them to employees of Alan's company and prominent buyers from some of the leading department store chains. Most of the evening Kalinda was kept very busy and away from Gavin.

Finally, Kalinda stood alone with Laura, discussing the intricacies of her business, when Alan joined them with Gavin. But at the first opportunity Laura and Alan excused themselves, leaving Kalinda and Gavin alone.

"Great party, isn't it," Gavin finally said matter-of-factly.

"Yes, it is," Kalinda agreed.

"You've made the big time. Congratulations!"

"It's about time you acknowledged the new licensee for your luggage line, Gavin," Kalinda stated coolly with a mocking look in her darkened eyes.

"You must be very proud of yourself, Kalinda—nothing stood in your way."

"If you mean your rude intrusion during my presenta-

148

tion, you're right! That was stooping pretty low to ruin my chances! But if you're also referring to my being intimate with you, using you to get what I wanted—you're damn wrong!"

"Kalinda, you always have the amazing knack of thinking the worst of me. I would never walk into your meeting late on purpose. I had an important overseas phone call that ran longer than expected."

"How convenient!" Kalinda snapped.

"As for your second accusation—what else am I supposed to think?"

"That's something that only you would think of!" she blasted back, but his shrewd eyes were distracted, gazing over her shoulder. Automatically Kalinda turned and followed his stare. A very short, portly man with a moustache standing with a group of men smiled and nodded at them.

Kalinda nodded and turned back to Gavin but his eyes were still glued to the moustached man.

"Know him?" Kalinda queried with an acid tinge to her voice, peeved at being ignored.

"Yes, he's a buyer," Gavin returned casually, but the keen look to his eyes alerted her to something.

"A prospective buyer for the luggage?" Kalinda asked eagerly.

"Could be," he returned, sounding somewhat annoyed.

"Why don't you introduce me?" she asked boldly.

"Sorry, but our business relationship is over. You're on your own!" His eyes now glared down at her, their resentment unmistakable.

"Sounds like you're a sore loser," Kalinda returned flippantly.

"That's what it's been all about, hasn't it, Kalinda? A

contest!" His words were spat out in a venomous voice but his eyes held more pain than anger and Kalinda suddenly became very weary of their fighting.

"I never thought of our relationship as a contest, Gavin, but obviously you did," Kalinda said simply in a quiet voice.

"I'll be right back," Gavin said sharply and walked past her.

Don't do me any favors, Kalinda thought to herself as her eyes followed him out of curiosity.

He sauntered over to the prospective buyer. They exchanged a few words and Gavin laughed, patting the man on his back. Then Gavin said something else and the man looked in her direction and smiled. Kalinda wondered who on earth he could be? He had an air of self-importance, even though his tie was slightly askew and he was wearing a loud plaid suit. As they walked toward her, Kalinda felt Gavin was smiling a little too broadly, but she overlooked it in her preoccupation with the stranger.

Reaching her, Gavin announced, "Kalinda, I'd like you to meet a good friend of mine from Texas. Ben Wilson. Ben, this is Kalinda Forrest."

"Howdy," he said in a deep Texan drawl.

"Hello," Kalinda returned politely as she detected a cigar stuck between his thumb and index finger.

"You sure are a good-looking woman," Ben declared as he gave Kalinda the once-over and smiled appreciatively.

What do we have here, a ladies' man? Kalinda thought to herself with a wry grin.

"Can I get you a drink, Ben?" Gavin asked very eagerly.

"No, no, I couldn't think of you doing that. Just steer

150

me in the direction of the watering hole," he stated in a booming voice and then added, "Either of you care for a drink?"

"No, thank you," Kalinda returned and Gavin shook his head, looking over and indicating the direction of the bar.

As soon as he was out of earshot, Kalinda turned to Gavin with an incredulous look. "Watering hole! Who *is* he?"

Gavin looked around to see if anyone was listening, then looked back to Kalinda. In a low tone, so as not to be overheard, he explained, "He's one of our biggest buyers. He covers all of the southwestern territory and deals with many of the most prestigious department stores."

"You mean like Neiman-Marcus?"

"How'd you guess?"

"I do know something about department stores!" Kalinda flared.

"He's a very important man and we wouldn't want anything to happen to ruin our relationship with him," Gavin told her in a patronizing way.

Kalinda glared at him. "If you're insinuating I don't know how to treat clients, you're crazy! I know how to handle important clients."

"I bet you do," he shot back with eyes of steel blue.

Kalinda ignored his remark, determined to prove herself, and challenged, "Just watch me. I'll have him eating out of my hand."

"Yeah, that's your style all right," Gavin declared as his serious expression was contorted by an ironic smirk.

Kalinda glared at him again. "That was only a figure of speech and you know it!"

151

"Better leave Wilson alone. He's out of your league," he said simply, without any emotion.

Puzzled as to whether he was warning her or putting her down, Kalinda retorted, "I can handle him and I can take care of myself."

"Sure about that? Not everyone is a nice guy like me," he stated, giving her a meaningful look.

At that moment, to Kalinda's dismay, the Texan returned.

"How come you Yankees don't have any Old Grand-Dad? I had to settle for that Johnny-come-lately brand of Wild Turkey," he declared with a roar and then puffed the cigar he'd been carrying around. "Sure I can't fix you up with a drink?" he asked Kalinda.

"No, thanks. I'm fine," she returned with a friendly smile. If she was going to win him over, she might as well start right away, Kalinda reasoned.

"I *know* you're fine," he declared, staring at her, making Kalinda feel very uneasy.

Kalinda felt as if the man's eyes were undressing her and suddenly wished she hadn't opened her big mouth to Gavin. If she hadn't, she could have promptly excused herself. Kalinda looked up at Gavin, hoping against hope he'd come to her rescue, but he was oblivious to her, his eyes focused on the crowd.

"There's Julie," Gavin stated while Ben and Kalinda followed his stare.

She was a tall, very thin, blonde. She was also very attractive and probably a fashion model.

"Excuse me," Kalinda heard Gavin say and she started to protest, but Gavin whispered into her ear, "If you thought *I* abused you! Let's see how you make out with this client. Good luck!"

"But, Gavin, you can't leave me . . ." But her words had fallen on deaf ears. Gavin had walked away.

What could she do? She wanted to leave but her feet remained glued to the spot. How could she leave gracefully without offending this important buyer!

"She's pretty looking," Ben drawled and Kalinda nodded, her eyes still on Gavin and his friend.

"Yes, she is," Kalinda voiced glumly, turning back to the man next to her. "Where're you from, Ben?" Kalinda inquired, trying to start a conversation, but her enthusiasm left much to be desired.

"Dallas. Ever been to Dallas?"

"No, I haven't but I've heard it's nice. Have you seen my luggage?" Kalinda suddenly asked, her face brightening with the idea of talking about her company.

"Did you lose your luggage? Terrible city, the muggers and all. Down South, we don't have those problems," he declared, taking a gulp of bourbon.

"No, I didn't lose my luggage," Kalinda stated with an incredulous laugh. Gavin hadn't even bothered to fill him in on who she was and about her work! He was unbelievable! "My partner and I designed the new Richards luggage line. I thought perhaps Gavin might have mentioned it to you," Kalinda explained flatly, her mind on Gavin, wondering just why he'd introduced her to Ben Wilson. Gavin's broad smile and his eagerness to get Ben a drink were totally out of character for him and should have been a tip-off to Kalinda. Yes, he had been up to something and I fell for it hook, line, and sinker, Kalinda thought, totally peeved at herself.

"No, he didn't. Gavin said he'd find me a party girl," Ben announced, interrupting her thoughts and looking directly into her brown eyes.

153

"He did, did he!" Kalinda declared with feigned surprise and glanced over in Gavin's direction with a blood-thirsty look.

Gavin's sharp eyes darted in her direction and caught her eye. Kalinda shot him a disgusted look, deciding she'd have to find a way to fix his wagon. To her chagrin, a beguiling smile decorated his face and he waved with a limp wrist. You think you're cute, don't you, Kalinda fumed to herself and gave him a proud twist of her head, turning back to the Texan.

The moment she looked at Ben, she knew what she was going to do. "Ben, why don't you go over and join Gavin. I think Julie's got an eye for you," Kalinda suggested in a very charming, convincing way.

"She does?" Ben declared, very excited by the news.

"Yes, go on, Ben," Kalinda urged.

"Don't mind if I do," Ben stated and took another puff on his cigar before moving in their direction.

Kalinda watched as Ben strolled over to Gavin and Julie and boldly tapped Gavin on the shoulder. Words were exchanged and Ben laughed, then he turned his attention toward Julie. Gavin turned and looked at Kalinda. She waved with a smug look on her face; he grinned in acknowledgment.

But her victorious feeling was short-lived as their eyes locked and held. Kalinda was suddenly reminded of that night in Damiens, which seemed centuries ago, when she was touched by his look and saw beneath the surface of Gavin Richards. Even then she probably had been a little in love with him, but hadn't known it until this very moment. And Kalinda was saddened. Instead of looking at each other from across a crowded room, playing cha-

154

rades, hurling accusations at each other, they should have been in each other's arms, sharing this special event.

A weariness overcame her and drawing her eyes away from Gavin, she surveyed the room. Most of the guests had already departed, except for a few engaged in talking and some couples dancing to the slow, rhythmic music. It was time for her to leave. Besides, she'd wanted to talk to Grace and it was still early enough to call her. Kalinda was anxious to reach her friend to tell her the good news about the luggage contract. She'd tried to call Grace several times during the past week, but each time she'd called either the line had been busy or there had been no answer. With that thought in mind, Kalinda said goodbye to the Richardses, Kate, and a few other people she'd met.

As she reached the door, Kalinda turned around for one last look, taking a mental photograph of the glittering ballroom with its glamorous occupants and soft music, to be preserved forever in her memory. Finally, her surroundings absorbed, Kalinda turned to leave, but the song the band was playing caught her attention and she froze. She recognized the tune. Ironically it was "The Twelfth of Never." Her vision was blurred momentarily as a flood of memories swept through her mind. Yes, she'd love Gavin forever and that's a long, long time, Kalinda thought sadly to herself.

"You aren't leaving without giving me a dance," she heard Gavin say and she looked with childlike eyes, totally taken off guard, in the direction of his voice. He smiled down at her. "I've even had them play our favorite song," he stated, taking her hand and leading her out into the center of the room, directly in front of the band.

Gavin swiftly took her into his arms and involuntarily

her body pressed against his firm chest, her cheek against his, as they moved slowly to the beat of the melody. The strength of his body and the sweet familiar fragrance of his aftershave aroused her senses, stimulating her desire for him.

"God, how I've missed your body coming alive against mine," he whispered as the warmth of his breath fanned across her cheek. "And you were leaving without me."

Kalinda's emotions were thrown into turmoil. She hadn't planned on this happening and she couldn't risk being alone with him again, especially knowing how he felt about her, that she'd used him. And even though she'd told him it wasn't so, he hadn't believed her. Her thoughts jammed and she had to put distance between them.

Pulling her head away from his, Kalinda stated freshly, "Really! I thought you were into models."

Gavin's features hardened. "At least they're not hot one minute and like ice the next! You'll have to forgive me though, I keep forgetting you're only into clients. Why'd you let Ben get away?" His voice had been honed to razor sharpness and Kalinda was cut to the quick.

"Terrific! Once you've gotten locked into something, you won't let go. And I've never done anything to make you believe that. And if that's the way you feel, why don't you go find your blond bombshell and dance with her!" Kalinda burst out. She broke his hold and bolted away, walking as fast as she could without drawing attention to herself. Once out of the mirrored door, Kalinda raced to the hatcheck room. Her icy hands fumbled into her bag for her check as she stood in line to retrieve her jacket. Finding it, Kalinda anxiously awaited her turn.

"Next," the woman finally said to Kalinda and she quickly produced her ticket.

Taking it, the hatcheck woman searched through the coats, matching up its number with that on a hanger.

"Here it is," the little woman said with a sigh and dragged it out. To her dread, it was Gavin's coat, not hers.

"Oh, I'm sorry but that's not mine," Kalinda declared immediately. "I guess the tickets got mixed up. Mine's the mink jacket, probably next to that coat."

The woman raised one eyebrow and gave her a skeptical gaze. "Can't hand out coats without tickets," she stated firmly, shaking her head, and moved away.

"Is this what you're looking for?" Gavin was smiling broadly, waving the claim check in his hand.

"Give me that!" Kalinda demanded as she leaped toward him, trying to grab the ticket.

"Now, now, no ticket, no coat!" he said in a tantalizing voice, quickly moving the ticket out of her reach, over her head.

"You deliberately mixed them up, didn't you!" Kalinda flared.

"You don't call me Big Red for nothing," Gavin returned with a chuckle.

"Cute!" was all she managed to say. He definitely had a way of getting under her skin.

The woman returned and Kalinda watched silently as Gavin handed her the claim check. She smiled appreciatively at him but gave Kalinda an obvious look of disapproval before turning to get her jacket. Typical! I come off like the heavy while the big lug comes off smelling like roses, Kalinda thought to herself with a frown. Tipping

157

the woman and taking the jacket, Gavin held it for Kalinda.

"I can help myself, thank you!" Kalinda snapped, reaching for her mink jacket.

"No, it's my pleasure," Gavin insisted with a sardonic ring to his voice and held the jacket firmly.

With a shrug of her shoulders, Kalinda gave up and slipped into it. Placing his hands on her shoulders, Gavin turned her around to face him.

"When are you going to stay and face things instead of always running away?" he said, looking deeply into her eyes.

"You've got it all wrong, Gavin. You're the one who doesn't like to deal with the truth. Now if you don't mind, I'd like to go home. And I have nothing more to say to you."

"I'll take you home."

"No, thanks. I can get a cab."

"I brought you here and I'll take you home," Gavin insisted, his eyes flickering dangerously.

"Fine, you can take me home. But that's all," she stated coolly.

"Don't be so presumptuous," he returned sarcastically, whipping his overcoat on.

"Look, you don't have to take me home!" Kalinda flared as she started to leave.

"I always finish what I start," Gavin stated, coming after her.

"Sounds like I'm some kind of business deal," she exclaimed, walking toward the steps.

As Gavin caught up with her, he accused, "Isn't that the way you treated me! What more do you want from me, Kalinda?"

158

Shocked, Kalinda paused at the top of the stairs and looked at him. Then she walked down the steps quickly as Gavin followed her. "Something you can't give me!" Kalinda cried.

"What's that?"

Without answering him, Kalinda continued along and pushed her way through the revolving door, Gavin right behind her. Once out into the biting wind, Kalinda clutched the top of her jacket.

"What is it you want that I can't give you?" Gavin demanded, his eyes sharp.

"I told you before. I don't want to be in a relationship with someone who can't trust me and can't make a commitment."

"Who says I can't make a commitment?" Gavin shouted back, only dealing with half her statement.

"See, you can't even *tell* me you trust me and you can't even say you *can* make a commitment! You have to answer me with a question. That proves you can't!"

"God, woman's logic!"

"And when all else fails bring out the chauvinist routine! Where's your car?" Kalinda asked, looking around angrily, tapping her foot.

"We have to wait for the parking attendant to come around! Kalinda, what happened? We had such a lovely time in Connecticut." His voice had softened and Kalinda was touched by the pleading look in his eyes. "Was I only a business deal to you?"

"Oh, Gavin, how can you even ask me that? I love you," Kalinda cried. "I keep trying to tell you and you *still* don't believe me. And I can't deal with this situation anymore!"

"Kalinda, I don't understand . . . you don't make

any sense," Gavin declared as a small smile threatened at the corner of his mouth, irritating Kalinda no end.

"Great! I just told you I loved you and all you can say is, I don't make sense!"

At that moment a cab pulled over to the curb, directly in front of them.

Spying it, Kalinda voiced, "Just go away, Gavin, and leave me alone! I can see myself home!" And Kalinda, without any further comment, walked over to the cab and got in, slamming the door behind her. The cab sped away, leaving Gavin standing there.

Later that evening Kalinda lay wide awake in her bed, her favorite comforter pulled up to her chin. Her mind was like a live wire, her thoughts whirling. She had called Grace to tell her the good news, only to learn her friend had slipped on ice and sprained her ankle and bruised her hip. And Grace's assistant was away on a two-week vacation in Mexico. Kalinda, on hearing the news, had immediately offered to come and work in her store and do anything else that was needed. Kalinda told her friend she'd try to be there on Saturday. She just had to tie up a few loose ends at her office tomorrow.

Only after she'd hung up the phone did Kalinda realize her planned trip to Edgartown was a blessing in disguise. She needed to get away to think, to be by herself. And the opportunity to be on Martha's Vineyard afforded her the time and space required to salve her aching heart. Why did she fall in love with him? He *still* didn't trust her— how could he think that she had been using him! And why wouldn't he listen to her when she told him the truth? He had to be just using it as an excuse—another manipulation to keep them apart. And even telling him

160

that she loved him wasn't enough for him to believe that he meant more to her than just a business deal.

Right from the beginning all the signs were there, all the warnings not to get involved with him. But, oh no, she hadn't listened. She had rushed blindly in, listening only to her heart. And her heart would pay dearly in the days to come for speaking out so boldly!

CHAPTER TEN

Cheerful and very feminine were the words that best described the atmosphere in Grace's tastefully decorated bedroom, with its lavender flowered wallpaper, ruffled canopy bed, pale blue lamps, a white vanity and chest of drawers, and various pieces of antique colonial furniture. Kalinda walked softly to the foot of Grace's queen-sized bed. How small and frail she looks, Kalinda thought, observing the sleeping woman, and her eyes filled with concern. A massive array of curls crowned her head like a silvery halo and a red blush brightened her pale cheeks. Grace was a woman who always took great pride in her looks and would never allow anyone to see her without makeup, not even if she was sick and confined to her bed. A small grin flashed across Kalinda's face. The rouge, no doubt, had been freshly applied for me, she thought, and she'd fallen asleep before I arrived.

Grace suddenly opened her eyes and a gentle smile came to her lips as she recognized Kalinda. "It's about time," Grace teased in a groggy voice and raised her head from her pillow.

"Here, let me help you," Kalinda quickly offered and moved to her friend's bedside, helping Grace slowly sit up. Kalinda lifted the pillow and propped it under her friend's head.

"That's fine, dear." The woman smiled, appreciating Kalinda's efforts. "What a dumb thing to do—go flying over ice. I guess I thought I was a spring chicken," Grace declared with a chuckle.

"You are a spring chicken," Kalinda stated with a smile, sitting in the antique wooden chair next to Grace's bed.

"Try telling that to these brittle bones," Grace piped with squinted eyes, patting her bruised hip. "My legs just can't keep up with my thoughts these days. I was anxious to get to the store. All the summer clothes are coming in and have to be unboxed, priced, and put on the racks. I had my mind on that and not where I was going."

"Well, don't worry about that. I'm here and I'll take care of everything. Just take care of yourself and get better," Kalinda ordered gently. "Can I get you anything?"

"No, nothing. Wilfred's been pampering me like an old hen. He's driving me crazy. Every time he looks at me, I'd swear he's sizing me up for a casket."

Kalinda laughed. "Grace, how can you say that about old Wilfred? You know he adores you and is terribly worried about you."

"I hate staying in bed and worse, I hate people like Wilfred fussing over me," she protested with a cantankerous sound to her voice. Kalinda smiled.

"It's only a few weeks, Grace; surely you can behave yourself that long."

163

With a wrinkled brow and pursed lips, the silver-haired woman shook her head slowly with an air of steadfast stubbornness. "Easy for you to say," she muttered. Then with a quick swat of her hand, Grace stated, "Enough of me. What about you and Gavin?"

Kalinda was taken aback by the frankness of Grace's unexpected question, but was touched by the concern in her eyes. What could she tell her friend? That she loved Gavin and probably would never see him again, except for maybe a brief encounter at Alan's office. No, she couldn't tell Grace that.

"There's nothing to tell," Kalinda finally said as she glanced down at the rug, for a moment, then looked back up to Grace.

"What happened?" her ex-mother-in-law asked as her eyelids suddenly became very heavy and tiredness etched her face.

"It didn't work out, that's all. And I'm fine," Kalinda quickly added, wanting to put Grace's mind at ease. "Look, you'd better get some rest and I'll unpack. Tomorrow you can fill me in on what has to be done in your store. Okay?" Kalinda asked.

Grace yawned. "All right, dear. The pain-killers the doctor gave me sure do make me sleepy. Promise to tell me all about your luggage," Grace added as her eyelids were slowly closing.

"I promise. Good night," Kalinda whispered affectionately. She stood up and bent over Grace, carefully adjusting her pillow and pulling her woolen blanket up.

As Kalinda tiptoed to the bedroom door, "Leave it open, dear—thanks for coming" were the faint words Kalinda heard just before quietly walking out into the hallway.

Kalinda walked into the colonial guest bedroom, with its low ceiling and antique furniture, and closed the door behind her. Shutting the door she gave in to her desperate need to be alone, her need to close out the world. Tears welled up in her eyes as the pain of losing Gavin washed over her again. She had told him she loved him and he hadn't believed her—hadn't trusted her. And maybe that made it easier for him to let her go. She had known all along he wanted to be free. And he had latched onto the one thing that would allow him to walk away. She would just have to be strong enough to put Gavin Richards out of her mind, once and for all. And spending time on this mystical island, the place that she loved and that had given her comfort, just had to heal her aching heart. Kalinda laid her head upon the pillow as silent tears streamed down her face.

Kalinda's first week in Edgartown crawled dreadfully by at a snail's pace. Her days were spent working in Grace's shop, rearranging the winter clothing with the new summer clothes, and her evenings with Grace, keeping her friend's spirits up and Wilfred out of her silver hair. She also stayed in constant touch with Kate, making certain her partner could handle the business alone. Kalinda was kept informed about all shipping schedules and returned all phone calls from her clients. Kate reassured her the company was running smoothly and for her to relax and enjoy her time with Grace, but Kalinda became more depressed each time she talked to Kate. Because each time she hoped there'd be a message from Gavin saying he'd misjudged her, and to her disappointment there wasn't one.

Each phone call to Kate only resulted in a painful realization that he really hadn't cared very much for her, hadn't really believed her when she tried to tell him the truth. As the days passed, her longing for him increased instead of diminishing. Constantly she wondered about him, what he was doing and if he ever thought about her. She was unable to keep him out of her mind. His strong, muscular body and his tender spirit had left their mark upon her, arousing a passion in her that she'd never forget.

It was early Saturday morning and Kalinda had a difficult time dragging her weary body from the warmth of her bed into the unfriendly chill in her room. She'd slept very little in Grace's home, and last night, spent tossing and turning, had been no exception. As usual her mind had been on Gavin, and again, during the wee hours of the morning, when everything's more magical, Kalinda had fantasized about sharing her life with Gavin. In her whimsical imagination it had been an exciting and very happy life filled with half a dozen carrottop kids. And she'd have Gavin and her work. She had imagined Gavin as a very loving husband, proud and supportive of her business accomplishments. But it had only been a wistful fantasy, stealing from her precious hours of sleep. And she'd awaken as she did this morning, feeling more exhausted and alone, with only the darkened circles under her eyes as a souvenir of her imagined love life with him.

The moment her feet hit the icy floor, Kalinda quickly dressed, pulling on a pair of woolen socks, her jeans, a sweat shirt, and finally her boots. She sped into the kitchen, where she gulped down a cup of black coffee under Wilfred's critical and disapproving eye. Kalinda threw on her down parka and went out the door. Walking at a brisk pace with an air of purpose, Kalinda passed many of the large white homes with their white fences built by the whaling captains of years gone by. And she recalled how intrigued she'd been as a child when she'd heard the stories of how the wives would wait with telescopes on the deck areas on the roofs of their homes, waiting for their husbands' ships to return. The deck area became known as a widow's walk. Oh great, tonight I'll probably have a nightmare about being married to Gavin and I'll be up on the widow's walk with my telescope, watching his ship come in when a treacherous storm threatens to knock it about, Kalinda thought with an ironic grin.

With that in mind she quickened her steps, making her way through the center of the sleepy village of Edgartown to Grace's shop. Because it was off-season, many of the shops were closed until after twelve on the weekends. But Kalinda wanted to get to work early because a shipment of merchandise had arrived the day before and she had to unpack the clothes, copy down their style numbers along with their descriptions, and take the list to Grace for pricing. Then price tags had to be attached to the merchandise and the clothing hung on the racks.

Hoping a delivery of suits Grace had been expecting from England might be delivered, Kalinda left the door of the shop open as she worked in the storage room. That way if she didn't hear the delivery man arrive, he could let himself in. Bending down on the floor, Kalinda attempted to make some order out of the clutter of cartons that filled the stockroom.

"I thought you sold luggage. Where's your luggage department?" were the sharp words that shocked Kalinda.

Her head jerked up and her fears were confirmed. Gavin towered above her, his masculine frame against the opened door. The wondrous sight of him caused her heart to flutter and a peculiar tremor circuited up her spine. But the cold look in his eyes and his large body hovering above her intimidated her and she quickly stood up.

"What are *you* doing here!" she finally managed to blurt out as she felt a rush of blood to her face.

"That's my question," Gavin declared in a harsh tone with a cock of his blond brow. Dark circles underscored his blue eyes, making them seem so pale. "Why'd you leave?"

"Grace needed my help and I needed to think."

"About what?"

"Me."

"That's par for the course!" The sarcasm in his voice was unmistakable.

"If you came here to badger me, you can leave," Kalinda stubbornly ordered, looking out the door in the direction she wanted him to go.

"Why the hell didn't you let me know you were leaving!"

In a daze, Kalinda turned her face to him. The look in his eyes was frightening—scorching! Gavin stood there regarding her with steely eyes as a ruddy flush crept up to color his left cheek. "Answer me!" he demanded.

He infuriated her. What had he expected! "What the hell difference would it have made?" she yelled as she tried to sweep past him, but he was too quick, too determined, and he moved, blocking her way.

"What is that supposed to mean? Are you playing games with me? I was really worried about you!"

For a moment Kalinda was speechless as Gavin's tall figure stood in front of her. She stared at him, stunned by the implication in his voice. He'd truly been worried about her, almost to the point of fear.

"I told you that I loved you and that I hadn't used you and you didn't believe me. You let me go without a word. And I thought it was over between us. I was hurting. Don't you see, I had to get away. To be by myself. To put myself together again."

As Kalinda spoke, she looked up into Gavin's face. It was now peaceful, his eyes filled with a misty, warm light.

"Oh, Kalinda," he cried as he moved closer to her. "You didn't have to leave."

"I did, Gavin. I have my career and you have your life. And you doubted me."

"But, Kalinda, I want you with me. And I was a fool to think that all I meant to you was a business deal and I'll never doubt you again. How can I convince you of that?" He was suddenly silent, but his eyes were active, as though going over something in his mind. Finally, he said, "Let's make a deal."

"You've got to be kidding!" Kalinda shot back. "I've got to get out of this hallway. I'm starting to get claustrophobic."

"Does being close to me bother you?" Gavin demanded with a knowing look to his eyes.

"Yes, but not the way you mean," Kalinda couldn't help but reply. "Come on," she said, leading him into the main part of Grace's store.

Gavin glanced around the room, noting its well-displayed merchandise, neatly and carefully arranged on shelves and racks. "Nice store," he said, his eyes distant.

"Yes, isn't it. And how's business with you?" Kalinda asked casually, trying not to be seduced again by his presence, by knowing he'd come to see her. He'd made a pretty speech but could she believe it? Did he finally trust her now and was he really going to make a commitment?

"Business is fine. The only thing that's wrong is, I'm without you."

Again ignoring the intimate quality of his voice, she changed the subject and quickly asked, "How'd you know I was here?"

"I called you at home because I didn't want to bother you at the office. I'd call you late at night and you weren't home. At first I thought you were just out, but then when I kept calling and there was no answer, I started to get worried. I woke up in the middle of the night thinking you were sick and in the hospital. I called Kate first thing the next morning."

"Kate? You talked to Kate?" Kalinda asked, surprised, and Gavin nodded. "She never told me you called."

"I asked her not to."

"Why?"

"Because if you knew I was coming, you might of run away again," he declared with an impish grin.

"I didn't run, I walked away from you," Kalinda stated, shaking her head, knowing he was getting the better of her.

"How about a date?" he suggested in an intimate tone.

"Is that the deal you were talking about before?" she returned.

"I'll tell you all about it on one condition—that you go to Lambert's Cove with me tonight for dinner," Gavin stated optimistically.

"How'd you know about that place?" Kalinda asked suspiciously.

"That's where I'm staying," he returned matter-of-factly.

"Why? Why are you staying there?" Kalinda questioned, tension and apprehension building in her voice. Her eyebrow rose, giving him a skeptical glance.

Gavin chuckled. "Because I've come here to seduce you and take you back with me."

Kalinda laughed dryly. "At least you're honest. I'll give you that much."

A serious expression crept across his face. He looked at her intensely, his blazing eyes boring into hers. "If seven o'clock is all right with you, I'll pick you up tonight at Grace's and prove to you how honest I really am. Bye," he said with a wink, turned, and sauntered out of Grace's store.

An apprehensive look darkened her face as she watched him disappear. What had she set herself up for? Though he'd admitted to being wrong, did that mean they would have a future together? And even *if* he really meant what he said about wanting her, was she building up false hopes only to be painfully separated from him again, Kalinda wondered with a weary heart.

The dinner was perfect in the old colonial house turned inn. Gavin was more at ease than she'd ever seen him. They talked a great deal and Gavin asked her to give him the weekend to prove how sorry he was and that he really wanted her, and she agreed to take him up on his deal. But as the evening wore on Kalinda became very quiet. It was more and more evident to her that the part of evening when lovers find comfort in each other's arms was approaching.

171

"Would you care for some more wine?" Gavin asked softly.

Kalinda nodded, her expression void of emotion. She was arrested by the brightness in his eyes as he said, "I like your hair that way. It looks sexy." He touched the curl that had come back to her unstraightened hair.

She started to say something clever but a sudden shakiness halted her words. Instead, she lowered her eyes and her gaze rested upon his rugged hand. Strong fingers cupped his drink and she was reminded of their touch caressing her body. A tingling sensation filled her veins as goose bumps feathered her skin and her emotions were reduced to a peaceful submissiveness.

She raised her unguarded eyes to his. Gavin, cool and in control, was studying her with a fixed, dominant stare. His physical being seemed to be electrically charged and she wondered what she could say to this virile man. Oh, how he had a way of affecting her! He had something special, a vulnerability mixed with a fierce, magnetic strength, which made her want to reach out and touch him, made her want to be close to him. A chill suddenly ran up her spine and she shivered, wondering what he could be thinking.

"Would you like to come up to my room . . . and see my etchings," he suggested with warm, inviting eyes.

More than you'll ever know, Kalinda thought to herself, and the thought of being with him again sent a quiver through her body.

Trying to be casual, Kalinda held her breath a brief moment before uttering, "Love to." Then suddenly she reached over and took his hand, his wonderful, masculine hand, and said, "Gavin, make love to me."

172

Gently he pulled her to him. "Come, darling, I want you to feel my love."

After paying the bill he led her slowly out of the restaurant and as they were met by the hostess, they nodded their thanks. They continued up the narrow steps to his room. She waited at the entrance as he entered and drew back the drapes. The moonlight drifted in, accentuating a large master bed. A jolt of electricity shot through her veins. How she wanted him!

"I want you to feel like you've never felt before," he whispered, taking her into his room and into his arms. "And I'm not going to stop until you cry out that you've never felt more like a woman, the woman I love."

He had said those magical words that her heart was longing to hear. Kissing him lightly upon his lips, Kalinda placed his hand on the top button of her expertly designed silk blouse.

"Undress me, darling," she said softly, pressing his hand, urging him.

"Oh, Kalinda," he sighed as he opened one button after another with a shaking hand. She nuzzled against his throat as she unzipped her slacks with one quick downward flick of her wrist. He helped her legs out of their confining material. Gavin parted her blouse and slid his hands inside, tracing the swell of her breasts. His hands moved down over her softly rounded stomach and Kalinda moaned softly.

He raised her mouth to his and she kissed his lips, savoring the tart aftertaste of Scotch. They kissed long and passionately and Gavin stirred against her body. He gently eased her down onto the bed. Kalinda took in his body as he began to undress, her eyes following his strong, muscular body that she loved to look at. Finally, his task complete, he sighed and stretched out next to her, his body warm as he took her into his arms.

"Don't ever leave me again," he said in a voice choked with emotion.

"I won't," she promised, her own voice catching in her throat.

Their lips met and their tongues churned together. His fingers stroked her body, slowly and carefully, awakening her smooth, soft skin. Little tremors followed the path of his fingers. She felt dangerously frail under his powerful touch, as though she would break into a thousand pieces at any moment. His mouth caressed her neck. Then his warm lips traced her collarbone on down to her breasts. Gavin let out a soft cry as her nipple became rigid under his touch.

His warm lips were on hers again and her arms were around him, her urgent, excited hands circling his back. Her body rose to such a pitch that she could no longer control the moans rising in her throat.

"I want you, darling," she whispered huskily. With urgent hands, she eased him over her.

Gavin entered her slowly as she cradled him in her arms. They rocked back and forth, gently at first, then Gavin's breath came in short, quick gasps as Kalinda matched him with hungry cries. He raised himself on his elbows and stared down at her with eyes that saw into her very soul.

"I love you, Kalinda," he cried with unveiled eyes.

"I love you too," she said as she pulled him down, close to her.

He began moving, driving harder, deeper, as a passionate groan rose in his throat. His excitement carried her to heights where she'd never been before and she went freely, lovingly. Her body rose and met his, exploding together again and again. At last with gasping moans, they tensed, bodies arched, and then relaxed into a calm, peaceful submission.

Everything was still as their bodies separated, lying next to each other. The only sounds were their deep, uneven breathing as Gavin reached over and took her hand.

"I want to marry you," he whispered gently. His eyes closed slowly and he fell into a deep sleep, little snoring sounds escaping from his mouth. But Kalinda didn't sleep. She stared up at the ceiling and thought. He had told her he wanted to marry her. His words had been what she most had wanted to hear, but the joy she'd expected was absent. Why had he so suddenly known that he wanted her to be his wife when only such a short time ago he hadn't even trusted her, hadn't even wanted a commitment? Had his words been spoken only out of the passion they just shared together, or had he been really certain? Kalinda glanced down at his sleeping, peaceful face. I couldn't bear to go through the pain of believing him only to find out that he'd change his mind because it was something he really wasn't ready for, Kalinda thought sadly to herself. But she would wait till morning to decide what she must do, she agreed to herself, laying her head on the pillow next to Gavin. And he would help her make that decision, she promised silently as she was gently lulled to sleep by the sound of his soft, even breathing.

But dawn came too early for Kalinda. She awakened with a headache and feeling out of sorts. Gavin was loving and warm, but Kalinda became distant, remembering her apprehension of the night before. She asked him to take her to Grace's store first to put the closed sign on the door so she could spend the time with him.

But when they arrived at the store, Gavin seemed anxious to talk to her. "When will you be coming back?" he asked, looking keenly into her eyes.

"I'm not certain," Kalinda returned, her eyes evasive. "As soon as I can."

"You are going to marry me, aren't you?"

Kalinda braced herself. She had to be strong. But he stood too close to her, weblike lines fanning out from the corners of his startling blue eyes. She had to move away from him. She spied a rack of skirts and quickly walked over to them, using the excuse to straighten one of the skirts that was sticking out. Then she turned back to him.

"Now that's better," she said with a smile, but there was no warmth in his eyes as he stood waiting for her answer.

"Gavin, I thought this over last night and I think we'd better wait." Her words were spoken carefully and slowly.

"Wait for what? We do love each other, don't we?"

"Yes, we do. But marriage is a much bigger commitment," Kalinda said.

"But I don't understand. Isn't that what you wanted? Isn't that why you left me? And doesn't my wanting to marry you prove that I trust you!" Gavin cried. There was a pained look in his eyes and Kalinda ached.

"I'd like to believe that's what it means. But you're right—I am the one who wants marriage. Not you. And I think you need the time to be sure you really want me."

"What do I have to do to prove to you that I'm sure. You said you'd give me the weekend, not just one night."

"Please, Gavin, go back to New York for a while. We both need the time to think. I understand how important your freedom is to you and I wouldn't want you to do something to please me that you would regret the rest of your life. I know what it's like to put aside what you really want for someone you love, only to lose yourself in the process. I don't want that for you or for me."

"Kalinda, I know you may not believe this, but I knew I loved you the first moment I saw you. And as I got to know you, I realized you were everything I wanted in a woman. Strong, independent, and yet very warm and giving. I just wanted to be sure about you. And when we came back from Connecticut and you withdrew from me, I really believed you'd only seen me as a ticket to success for your company. All the doubts I'd pushed aside came flooding back. But when we were in bed last night, you made me feel loved and wanted, again. I knew you couldn't fake what you felt for me. So, you see, darling, I don't need any time to think. I love you and I want you to marry me. What do I have to do to make you understand that?"

His eyes were warm and misty and Kalinda's heart went out to him. But the memory of her own divorce and the pain she'd felt with Gavin still haunted her and she wanted him to be positive his proposal was based on his desire for a lifelong commitment for her, instead of sexual passion that could quickly die with the passing of time.

"Gavin," Kalinda finally said, "please give us some time. It's important. What's a little time if we love each other?"

His eyes turned steely blue. "Maybe you're the one

who's not certain!" he flared. "I guess you're still frightened to take a chance."

"That's not true! I told you I loved you and you know I do," she stated loudly, trying to break into his defenses, which were beginning to shut her out.

Gavin turned toward the door.

"Gavin, won't you at least look at me. I said I loved you. I'm just not certain of your commitment, that's all."

He turned back to her. One side of his full mouth lifted into a sardonic half-smile. "Maybe you don't love me enough," he said simply, turning away from her. He left, the door slamming behind him.

His voice still rang in her ears but he'd already gone. Kalinda had to be right about giving him more time. From all their previous conversations, he'd always been totally against remarrying again. It's a risk sending him away, Kalinda thought hopelessly to herself, but if he's really ready for marriage he will come back. But so much had been said, she hoped he'd understood that she'd sent him away because she loved him and she had to be certain of his love for her. Her eyes suddenly clouded up with a misty film. I hope I'm right—he just has to come back! Kalinda thought sadly. Then she quickly pushed her thoughts toward the work that had to be done in Grace's store. Only one more week until Grace's assistant returned and Kalinda would be back in New York to find out what her destiny would be.

CHAPTER ELEVEN

Hot streams of water poured over her tired body, the heat massaging every pore and reviving her. But her mind was still weary, so many thoughts disturbing its rest. It was incredible how quickly one could seem so different, in only a few weeks, Kalinda thought to herself with a frown.

She'd returned to New York over a week ago and had been kept very busy at work, but she'd received no word from Gavin. In her mind she'd gone over every detail of their last meeting and Kalinda was still positive she'd done the right thing for the both of them. She loved Gavin terribly and wanted to be with him, but only if he meant everything he'd said about making a commitment to her and trusting her. But she missed him, and as the days passed she began to fear that she might not hear from him.

Kalinda had just stepped out of the shower when the phone rang. Grabbing a towel, she quickly ran to answer before it stopped ringing.

She raised the receiver to her ear. "Hello, Kalinda," the masculine voice said.

"Hello," she returned, not having the foggiest idea who could be calling her so early in the morning.

"This is Alan. I hope I didn't catch you at a bad time."

"No, not at all, Alan. I was just getting ready to go to work."

"I hope you don't mind, but I was wondering if you could come into my office this morning, perhaps before you go to work. I have a favor to ask you."

His voice had a strained sound to it and Kalinda immediately wondered what was wrong. "Sure, Alan, no problem," she returned in a calm, pleasant voice, even though her nerves were playing havoc with her stomach.

"Thanks, see you in a little while. Bye."

There was a click at the other end of the line and Kalinda slowly put the receiver down. Her mind was racing, wondering what on earth he could possibly want. She just hoped it didn't have anything to do with the samples. Maybe it was Gavin? Could something be wrong with him? Not wanting to play any more guessing games that were worse than Russian roulette, Kalinda quickly dried herself off and proceeded to get dressed.

Jerking to a stop, the cabbie flipped off the meter.

"Three fifty!" he announced in an impersonal voice.

Kalinda paid him and stared up at the tall building directly across from her. She opened the cab door and eased herself out, closing the door behind her. Kalinda took a deep breath, exhaling slowly, then an even bigger breath, needing the time to calm down. Without further hesitation she walked over to the building, pushed

180

through the swinging door, and stepped onto the elevator that would carry her up to Alan's office.

The elevator door opened and Kalinda stepped out with apprehension. The door closed sharply behind her.

The moment she walked into the reception area, the receptionist looked up with a smile and said, "He's expecting you, Ms. Forrest. Go right in. Know the way?"

"Yes, I do. Thank you," Kalinda returned and with more determined steps walked through the corridor, past the many offices. She paused at the closed door of Alan's office and suddenly wondered if Gavin would be there. And his beautiful blue eyes came to mind. Would they greet her coldly with anger, or with understanding? Straightening her shoulders, Kalinda placed her hand on the doorknob, noting her palms were perspiring slightly, and slowly turned the doorknob.

"Kalinda, thanks for coming so early," Alan stated the moment he saw her.

The friendly tone of his voice immediately relaxed her.

"Is there anything wrong?" Kalinda quickly asked, not wanting to be kept in the dark any longer.

"No, of course not. Oh, I'm sorry," he said as he noted the look of concern in her eyes. "I should have explained over the phone, but in my hurry to get the problem solved, I just asked you to come over. Please sit down," he offered.

Maybe I should hear the news standing, Kalinda thought with the feeling of dread growing inside her by the minute. But her legs weakened and Kalinda automatically sat in the chair next to Alan's desk.

"How've you been?" Alan asked.

"Fine," Kalinda returned calmly, becoming very impatient with his indirect approach.

181

"Well, I'll get right to it."

I wish you would, you're driving me crazy, Kalinda wanted to say but didn't.

"The Stanley Cup play-offs are tonight." He hesitated.

"Yes?" Kalinda asked, urging him on. The suspense was killing her!

"Well, Laura and I were supposed to go. And unfortunately I can't make it and I was wondering if you could fill in for me?"

"At a hockey game?"

Her voice echoed her surprise and her face must have expressed her dislike of the game, for Alan let out a loud roar. "Come on, Kalinda, hockey games aren't that bad."

"Is that why you're not going?" Kalinda teased with a nod of her head.

Alan's eyes sparkled. "Well, what do you say?"

Kalinda studied him, wondering if she should tell him the truth. Well, here goes nothing, she decided and declared, "Alan, I hope you don't mind me telling you this, but I hate hockey. Why don't you ask Gavin? I'm sure he'd love to go."

"You kidding? He's probably had his ticket for two years. It'd be a shame for the ticket to go to waste. And more important, Laura will be waiting for me at the game. I've tried to call her at home but I think she's already left for the city. I'm just afraid she might get tied up shopping and forget to call me, thinking she'll see me at the game. I'd hate for her to go to the game by herself," he said with imploring eyes.

He would have to put it that way!

"And the game's tonight?"

"Yes," he said simply but his eyes were alive with an expectant gaze. Boy, he and Gavin are becoming more alike every day, Kalinda thought with dismay, knowing she was boxed into a corner and couldn't refuse him.

"I wouldn't want Laura to go by herself either," Kalinda stated, still dreading the event. Only she knew her major objection to going to the hockey game. She wanted to avoid returning to a place where a memory had been made with Gavin.

"Thanks, Kalinda. I knew you'd help me out," Alan was saying as she blankly stared at him, her thoughts on Gavin. Alan reached into the breast pocket of his jacket and took out a ticket. "Here you go," he said in a very pleased voice.

"Thanks, Alan, wouldn't want this to go to waste," she said with a smile, taking the ticket from his outstretched hand. Catching the time on his watch, Kalinda declared, "Oh, boy, I'd better get going. I have an appointment at the office in half an hour."

"Have a good time," he called after her as Kalinda was on her way out the door.

Holding her ticket stub in her hand, Kalinda carefully made her way down the steps, searching for the seat that matched the number on her ticket. Cheers and yells went up from the crowd around her as the Rangers and the Boston Bruins swished across the ice. Finally, she spied the row and seat number and quickly walked to her seat. Luckily it was the second one over from the aisle, the first one empty, and Kalinda could sit down easily without disturbing any of the fans. Once into her seat, Kalinda looked around for Laura. But Alan's wife was nowhere to be found. The empty seat on the aisle had to belong to her. It had surprised Kalinda to be the first one there and she hoped nothing had happened to deter Laura from coming. Just then a loud roar went up from the crowd and Kalinda placed her hand on her forehead. A headache was threatening. A fight between players of opposing teams had broken out on the ice and all the fans around her stood up, watching with bloodthirsty eyes. But Kalinda remained seated, rubbing her head, and wondered how she could ever have agreed to attend this bone-crushing, animalistic spectacle. Kalinda suddenly thought she sensed a movement next to her and she felt relieved. Laura had finally arrived.

She looked over with a smile upon her face and exclaimed, "I thought you—" But her words froze. "It's you," she managed finally in a squeaky tone, her voice still not restored to its proper resonance.

Gavin sat next to her with his bushy brows raised and a puzzled expression on his face.

"Is that you?" he said, totally baffled.

"What are *you* doing here? What happened to Laura?" she demanded with a suspicious look in her dark eyes.

"*I* was supposed to be meeting Laura," Gavin retorted, resenting her accusatory tone.

"But Alan asked *me* to meet her."

"He asked *you?*" Gavin posed and Kalinda nodded with a sharp, positive jerk of her head. "He asked me too," he stated, then paused as though thinking over their predicament. Gavin suddenly chuckled and slapped his leg.

"There's nothing funny about this," Kalinda spat out in her most sarcastic voice.

"Don't you see," Gavin started, still smiling, "it was my little brother's way of bringing us together. Had to be. He and Laura have been so concerned about us. So they must've thought this up to trick us into being together.

184

And they knew us so well! They knew I'd never pass up a ticket to a Stanley Cup game and you'd never"—he paused for a moment, a wicked glint in his eyes, and then added—"pass up a business obligation."

Just then applause was heard and the crowd seated itself, while Gavin's awful deduction sank into Kalinda's thoughts.

"Oh, great!" she mumbled with a scowl upon her face.

Gavin regarded her with an annoyed gaze. "Look, don't act like you're the only one who's been duped!"

"Well, I'm not going to sit here another minute!" Kalinda declared, quickly grabbing her coat and standing.

"That's a typical thing you'd do!" Gavin yelled at her.

"Hey, lady, would you sit down!" a loud, gruff voice said, and Kalinda turned around to the crowd behind her to find out who'd yelled at her, but to her dismay all eyes were glued to the game.

So she turned back to Gavin and asked in a nasty voice, "What's that?"

"To go and waste a perfectly good ticket to the play-offs! Do you know how many guys were dying to come tonight!"

"Oh yeah, well I'm not one of the guys, or haven't you noticed!"

"I've noticed all right!"

"Hey, we want to see the game! Will ya sit down or get out!" yelled another angry fan.

Gavin's eyes squinted and a serious expression graced his face. Quickly standing next to Kalinda, he yelled back, "Hey, you can't talk to my wife like that!"

"Wife!" Kalinda exclaimed in a very surprised yet pleased voice and looked up at Gavin with adoring eyes. But catching herself, and relieved that his eyes had been focused on the fans behind her and not on her, Kalinda turned to the fans and yelled, "Don't listen to him! I'm not his wife!"

"Wife or not, will ya sit down!" a burly-looking man in a plaid hunting jacket yelled.

Another fan, much younger and with dark-rimmed glasses, yelled, "Hey, buddy, what's going on? Is she your wife or not?"

"She's going to be," Gavin yelled. "Just watch and see!" Turning his magnificent blue eyes to Kalinda, he asked, "What about it, will you please marry me? Will you finally believe me that I want to spend the rest of my life with you? And that I am so sure that I'd bet my life on it."

Kalinda stared at him, not believing her ears. Proposed to at a hockey game, could it be true? she wondered, studying his face for the slightest change, a shift of his eyes or a twitch in his cheek, making certain it wasn't a joke.

"Kalinda, I love you. I want you with me. Can't you get that through your silly head. I want you . . . I want you to be my wife. And you were right to send me away, because I found out something very important to me. Do you know what that was?"

"No," Kalinda returned softly.

"I found out that I can't live without you. And that you're the only person in the world I really trust. You're the only person in the world I'd trust with my life. I want you, Kalinda. But I want you to come to me willingly, without any doubts about me anymore. And if you're with me, it's because there isn't any place on earth that you'd rather be than at my side."

186

His eyes held hers. There was an unbelievable softness that she'd never seen before.

"Well?" Gavin asked. "Will you?"

"Say you'll marry him, lady, so we can watch the game!" The words broke the magic spell and made Kalinda's face light up with a broad smile that almost cracked her face. Tears streamed down her cheeks.

"Oh, Gavin, of course I will!" she cried, wrapping her arms around his neck and kissing him.

Cheers and applause went up from the crowd and Kalinda and Gavin broke apart, looking sheepishly down at the fans.

"What do you say we go back to my place and let these kind folks go back to watching their game," he suggested with a smile and took Kalinda's hand.

Another cheer went up from the crowd as one of the fans yelled, "Right on! Now he's talking!"

Kalinda and Gavin laughed as they ran up the stairs amid the roar of the crowd.

"Are you sure you don't mind missing the game?" Kalinda cried teasingly above the loud noise as they reached the top of the stairs and were about to go out the exit.

"I know you'll find this impossible to believe, Kalinda," Gavin exclaimed as they reached the escalator and stepped on, "but there are some things more important than a hockey game. . . . But not many." He then whispered in a seductive tone, "I can think of *one* right now."

Gavin shifted his weight and his arm brushed against Kalinda's. The warmth of his vibrant body permeated her silk blouse and scorched her skin, sending a thrilling current through her body.

"Your place or mine?" Kalinda posed in a low, deep voice matched with her intimate, velvety eyes.

"To mine," Gavin answered without missing a beat.

"Why?"

"Because I want you to see where we're going to live," he replied with an impish grin.

"Got it all figured out?" she said with a laugh as they stepped off the escalator, shrugged into their jackets, and walked over to the taxi stand.

"And just think, it's right around the corner from your favorite place."

"Damiens! Oh, no!" Kalinda cried. "I guess I've picked a real winner!"

A cab pulled up and Gavin opened the door. "Speaking of winners, maybe we'll get home in time to turn on the TV and catch the end of the game," he said with a wicked glint in his eyes.

"Oh no you don't!" Kalinda exclaimed loudly, giving him a big shove, and a look of feigned fear crossed Gavin's face as she continued to push him into the cab. Kalinda jumped in beside him and slammed the door closed. "I've got other plans for you tonight," she declared, kissing his lips lightly.

"Where to?" the cabbie asked, impatiently.

"Twenty Sutton Place South," Gavin said automatically. He looked at Kalinda with bewilderment, with wonderment in his eyes. "I love you," Gavin whispered.

"I love you too, Gavin."

The battered yellow cab bounced over potholes as it carried them up Eighth Avenue toward their destination. A light snow had begun to fall, but Kalinda didn't mind. She was wrapped in her lover's arms. Snow in April, how appropriate, she murmured to herself. It fit right in with the scheme of things for this unusual evening with its series of unlikely events—being proposed to at a hockey game, being together with Gavin again, and having a future with him. Life was so full of surprises, Kalinda thought to herself, as a smile danced upon her face and she turned her waiting lips to Gavin.

Look for Next Month's
CANDELIGHT ECSTASY ROMANCES®:

Candlelight Ecstasy Romances™

$1.95 each

CANDLELIGHT Ecstasy Supreme

☐ 37 **ARABIAN NIGHTS,** Heather Graham..................................10214-6-28

☐ 38 **ANOTHER DAY OF LOVING,** Rebecca Nunn.....................16789-2-12

☐ 39 **TWO OF A KIND,** Lori Copeland.......................................19082-7-10

☐ 40 **STEAL AWAY,** Candice Adams...17861-4-29

☐ 41 **TOUCHED BY FIRE,** Jo Calloway..19015-0-12

☐ 42 **ASKING FOR TROUBLE,** Donna Kimel Vitek....................10334-7-15

☐ 43 **HARBOR OF DREAMS,** Ginger Chambers...........................13446-3-14

☐ 44 **SECRETS AND DESIRES,** Sandi Gelles................................17675-1-17

$2.50 each

At your local bookstore or use this handy coupon for ordering:

DELL READERS SERVICE—DEPT. B392B
P.O. BOX 1000, PINE BROOK, N.J. 07058

Please send me the above title(s). I am enclosing $_____ (please add 75¢ per copy to cover postage and handling.) Send check or money order—no cash or CODs. Please allow 3-4 weeks for shipment.

Ms./Mrs./Mr._____

Address_____

City/State_____ Zip_____